Every love story is a ghost story.

—David Foster Wallace

FROM
THE
SHADOWS

FROM THE SHADOWS

JUAN JOSÉ MILLÁS

TRANSLATED BY THOMAS BUNSTEAD
AND DANIEL HAHN

Bellevue Literary Press
NEW YORK

First published in the United States in 2019 by
Bellevue Literary Press, New York

For information, contact:
Bellevue Literary Press
90 Broad Street, Suite 2100
New York, NY 10004
www.blpress.org

From the Shadows was originally published in Spanish in 2016
as *Desde la Sombra* by Seix Barral.

Text © 2016 by Juan José Millás

Translation © 2019 by Thomas Bunstead & Daniel Hahn

This is a work of fiction. Characters, organizations, events, and places
(even those that are actual) are either products of the author's imagination
or are used fictitiously.

Library of Congress Cataloging-in-Publication Data
Names: Millás García, Juan José, 1946– author. | Bunstead, Thomas,
    translator. | Hahn, Daniel, translator.
Title: From the shadows / Juan José Millás ; translated by Thomas
    Bunstead and Daniel Hahn.
Other titles: Desde la sombra. English
Description: First edition. | New York : Bellevue Literary Press, 2019.
Identifiers: LCCN 2018060792 (print) | LCCN 2018061540 (ebook)
    | ISBN 9781942658672 (ebook) | ISBN 9781942658665 (pbk. :
    alk. paper)
Classification: LCC PQ6663.I46 (ebook) | LCC PQ6663.I46 D4513 2019
    (print) |DDC 863/.64--dc23
LC record available at https://lccn.loc.gov/2018060792

Bellevue Literary Press would like to thank all its generous
donors—individuals and foundations—for their support.

 This publication is made possible by the New York State
Council on the Arts with the support of Governor Andrew
M. Cuomo and the New York State Legislature.

This project is supported in part by an award
from the National Endowment for the Arts.

Book design and composition by Mulberry Tree Press, Inc.

Bellevue Literary Press is committed to ecological stewardship in our book
production practices, working to reduce our impact on the natural environment.

♾ This book is printed on acid-free paper.

Manufactured in the United States of America

First Edition

1 3 5 7 9 8 6 4 2

paperback ISBN: 978-1-942658-66-5

ebook ISBN: 978-1-942658-67-2

PART ONE

1

SERGIO O'KANE was asking Damián Lobo which sea creature he identified with most.

"A shark, perhaps? . . . A sardine?"

"Definitely not a shark," said Lobo. "I'm not aggressive like that. I get kind of squeamish. Not a sardine, either. I don't know . . . maybe a moray eel?"

"*A moray eel.* And why is that?"

"It's quite shy, good at blending in, lives in tropical waters. And I can't stand the cold."

Sergio O'Kane was not real; he existed only in Damián Lobo's imagination, as a mechanism for conversing with himself. Damián told him everything he was thinking, usually as he was thinking it, in the form of an imaginary televised interview, which began the moment he got out of bed and stopped only once he'd gotten back into it. The interview was being broadcast globally, with simultaneous translations in non-Spanish-speaking countries. Lobo imagined it as being filmed in front of a studio audience while also going out live, with stratospheric viewing figures.

To begin with, O'Kane had been nothing but a voice inside his head, with neither outward form nor a story of his own. Over the years, however, Damián Lobo had gradually supplied him with a physical appearance and a fully realized biography. A native of Madrid, O'Kane was the son of a North American diplomat—hence the surname. He was in his mid-forties now, fair, five foot eleven, and, though slim, he had a very slight gut. He favored dark suits in combination with white shirts and somewhat extravagant ties, complete with gold tie clip. O'Kane always fastened the top button of his suit jacket when getting up from a chair, and unfastened it when about to sit down, an apparently casual gesture whose elegance Damián found particularly intriguing.

He had a very striking face, in part because of his eyes, which were yellow, and his wide mouth, whose fleshy lips parted to reveal a seemingly larger than average collection of teeth. His nose, a proper and nicely proportioned nose, went unnoticed in between these accidents of facial design. His forehead, which was broad and smooth, extended up into a receding hairline, which, far from hiding, he flaunted, with his hair scraped straight back.

"So," said O'Kane, "you're still on welfare two months after being fired—pitilessly, unceremoniously—from the job you worked in for twenty-five years."

"The job I started at eighteen," said Damián.

"I'm sure that must have been very difficult for you. Tell us, if you don't mind, what are your views on the heartlessness of today's capitalism?"

Damián Lobo pondered for a moment before explaining that the capitalist system had been to his life as water was to the fish that swam in it.

"By which I mean, I've never understood the environment. Just as an octopus doesn't need to understand the ocean to live in it."

"So, Señor Lobo, just to continue with the metaphor: In this particular ecosystem, which sea creature would you say you identify with most? A shark, perhaps? . . . A sardine?"

"Definitely not a shark," said Lobo. "I'm not aggressive like that. I get kind of squeamish. Not a sardine, either. I don't know . . . maybe a moray eel?"

The studio audience laughed. They often laughed when Damián spoke, even when what he said had not been obviously funny. But if he imagined them laughing, they laughed. They didn't have a choice in the matter.

While the imaginary interview with O'Kane continued in Damián's mind, he brought his cup of tea to his lips but found it still too hot to drink. He was sitting in a dark, narrow café, at the end of the bar, a good way from the rest of the clientele, like a moray eel hiding in a seabed crevice all its own. He had just come from lunch with his father and sister at their house in Arturo Soria, and had decided to stretch his legs before taking the subway home.

O'Kane's mentioning the heartlessness of capitalism took Damián back to the family meal, which he began to describe to his imaginary interviewer as he waited for the tea to cool.

"So my older sister is Chinese," he said. "And she and my father live together."

"How did that come about?" asked O'Kane.

"Her living with my father?"

"No, her being Chinese."

"Oh. My parents adopted her as a baby, having been unable to conceive. But then a couple of years later they did manage it, and I showed up."

"So they weren't trying for you?" asked O'Kane. "You were . . . a surprise?"

"That's right, I was a surprise."

The studio audience was still on tenterhooks. There were probably people tuning in everywhere, streaming in, like fish into a trawler's net. Damián

Lobo and Sergio O'Kane, both of them able to sense the bump in interest, acted naturally. The presenter looked into one of the cameras, granting it a close-up of those yellow eyes, with their little flecks and flares like solar storms. Breaking off, he turned back to his interviewee and, with an encouraging nod, urged him to go on.

"Like I said," Damián Lobo continued after a dramatic pause, "my Chinese sister's two years older than I am, so when I was fourteen, she was sixteen, and already very well developed."

Murmurs in the audience suggested imminent laughter—or widespread smiling at the very least. Damián Lobo, catching Sergio O'Kane's approving look, saw immediately where he needed to take the story next.

"And so, if you can imagine, there I was, right in the throes of adolescence, and her really, you know, *developing*. . . . She used to come out of the bathroom with nothing on but a skimpy towel, or she'd walk straight through the living room half-dressed. . . ."

"And you didn't find it troubling that it was your sister who was acting in this way?" said Sergio O'Kane, cutting across the swell of laughter in the studio.

"Well, on paper she was my sister, but it wasn't

as if she had come out of the same womb as I did, or as if my father's sperm had anything to do with her coming into being. On top of that, she was a different ethnicity from me, so in a way that made us even more unrelated. Given all of that, I don't think you can really call my desires incestuous. Or hers."

"She, too, felt an attraction?"

"I'm not sure if it was an attraction; it's just that ever since I was young, she'd always played with my penis."

Laughter erupted, and this time the presenter did nothing to quell it. Damián, meanwhile, sat stony-faced, as he always did whenever the audience found his answers funny. He was well aware it made the whole thing funnier if he kept a straight face. The show was bound to be going viral right about now, he thought.

"She started playing with your penis. . . ." repeated Sergio O'Kane.

"Yes, as far back as I can recall, I have memories of her telling me to drop my pants so she could play with it. Sometimes she came into my bedroom and took my pajamas off herself. She'd take it out, hold it out one way, then another, squeeze it in her hands, put it in her mouth. . . ."

Again the audience roared with laughter, drowning Damián out, and this time, while continuing to look as though he hadn't said anything funny, he added a touch of surprise—a go-to expression of his—as if to say he had no idea why people were laughing.

Sergio O'Kane, himself struggling not to laugh, finally calmed the audience, and Damián Lobo continued.

"She was always asking to come to the bathroom with me so she could hold it while I had a pee. She was obsessed."

"What did your parents say?"

"They never got wind of it. She always chose her moments."

"And what did you think?"

"Nothing. She started playing with it when I was tiny, so for me it was simply part of normal life."

"So she just went on doing it?"

"Yes, though as I got older, the consequences changed, naturally."

Now the laughter was rising intermittently, the audience pausing each time he began to speak, eager not to miss a thing.

"Now I'm wondering what this has got to do with what we were talking about," said O'Kane.

"You mentioned the heartlessness of capitalism, and that took me back to the lunch I had with my father and sister earlier today."

"Really?"

"The thing is, I can't remember how old I was exactly, twelve or thirteen possibly, but a moment came when my Chinese sister—her name's Desirée, by the way—started referring to it as my *kindhearted penis*."

This time, the presenter was the first to burst out laughing, followed by the members of the audience, who were beside themselves. Damián looked around uncomprehendingly, glancing back and forth between the camera operators and other crew, as if waiting for someone to explain the joke.

"So," said O'Kane, wiping away tears, "you've got a kindhearted penis. The idea presumably being that other people *don't* have kindhearted penises? Anyone in particular, do you think?"

"My father, I guess," Damián Lobo said uncertainly. "Maybe men in general."

He spoke the last part so solemnly that it plunged the audience into a silence just as intense as the laughter that had gone before.

"Well, I won't ask you to show us," said O'Kane eventually, trying to lighten the mood, "but I'm imagining something must have made her think of your penis as kindhearted."

"Something to do with having a nice face, I guess."

"Your sister?"

"No, my penis."

Again the audience started to howl, and O'Kane looked relieved, pleased to be back on familiar ground.

"Sorry about the laughter," he said once the audience had recovered. "It's just that I don't think we've ever had anyone on the show talking about penises with kind hearts before, or without kind hearts, for that matter."

The interview was going very well, in Damián's estimation. The only problem now would be how to top this climax. So he decided to inject a new note of drama, bring things down to earth a little.

"If my father saw this, he'd die of shame."

"Oh?" said O'Kane.

"He hates trashy TV. He only watches Canal+. He's subscribed ever since it first launched."

"And so to him the conversation we're having would be trashy?"

"Absolutely. Because of the subject matter, but also because we're discussing it in a shallow way."

"Why don't you tell us a little about your father?"

"He's a university professor as well as a renowned movie critic. An intellectual. He lives in a house full of books—books that always frightened me as a child."

"And why would you say that was?"

"Just the feeling that, every time I went near them, they seemed to call out to me to read them."

"You mean metaphorically, I guess?"

"No, not at all. I could hear their little voices whispering, 'Read me, please read me' as I walked by. Actually, it was just my father, who, as I passed the bookshelves, used to hide in one corner of his library, doing different voices. 'Read me, please read me.' I still hear it to this day, whenever I go anywhere near a book."

"Did you find certain books more frightening than others?"

"I always tried to avoid the nineteenth-century Russian section. The 'Read me' whispers there always sounded guttural, kind of tormented."

"And did you read any of them?"

"Never. I don't read anything but user manuals and instruction booklets."

"Instructions for what?"

"Anything and everything. Electrical domestic appliances, for example, but anything mechanical, really. I also love the rule books that come with board games."

This answer went down particularly well, and Sergio O'Kane took the chance to announce a commercial break. Damián Lobo returned to the counter in the café, where his tea was now cool enough to drink. He thought about the reception in the newspapers around the world the next morning. Reviews that would even transcend the "Culture" section and make it onto the front page; it had happened before. READ ME, PLEASE was a pretty eye-catching headline.

He finished his tea just as the commercials were coming to an end, and took himself back to the TV studio to carry on telling the world his story. After the lunch, he said, his father had fallen asleep in front of a Canal+ interview between Iñaki Gabilondo and a famous movie director.

"My father adores Iñaki Gabilondo," he said, "because—"

"Sure," O'Kane said, interrupting him, as if jealous of the well-known journalist, "but what about your mother? You've been surprisingly quiet about her."

"My mother was like an extension of my father; that's how I always saw her. My father was to her as Iñaki Gabilondo was to him. She died about ten years ago, but before that she taught chemistry in a public high school. She was a good teacher, I think, but the moment she got home, she fell in with whatever my father was up to—she sort of blended in; you couldn't really tell she was there. I believe my father wanted her dead so he could be alone with my sister, who, by the way, is Chinese."

"So you're saying your father wanted to be alone with your sister?"

"I am, but I'd rather not go into it."

In order to assuage the obvious disappointment of both his interviewer and their audience, Damián Lobo began describing how after lunch, as their father nodded off in front of the television, he and his sister had shut themselves away in her bedroom.

"To play with the kindhearted penis?" asked O'Kane with a smile.

"Yes," said Damián. Then, to the audience's delight, he launched into an account of the sexual acts the siblings had partaken in while their father slept.

As Damián began describing his Chinese sister's vulva and vagina, O'Kane must have heard a voice in his earpiece, and he seamlessly changed the subject.

"So tell us, what was the job you got fired from?"

"Capital goods. I was in charge of maintenance," said Damián.

"Looking after sockets, plumbing, that kind of thing?"

"Clearly, it's an area you don't know much about,

Señor O'Kane. To run a maintenance team, especially in this day and age, one has to be extremely
technically capable."

"And how did you come to be doing such a job?"

"I joined the company when I was very young,
as an apprentice, because, to my father's dis-
pleasure, instead of going to university, I went
straight into the world of work. I was very good
with my hands, and trained as an electrician. So
I learned on the job, you see. I've had young engineers come and work under me, a whole moun-
tain of theoretical knowledge in their heads but
completely unable to problem-solve when something needs an immediate answer. And anyway,
when I was starting out, there weren't the same
academic requirements as today."

At this point, Damián exited the interview—for
some reason, he was having trouble concentrating
on his daydreams—and returned to the café. It was
busier now, with a mass of people crowding around
the far end of the bar, by the door. Again he saw
himself as the moray eel hidden in the coral—lying
in wait for some prey, or protecting itself from a
predator of its own.

"So what did you do in your job?" said O'Kane's
distant voice, from the other dimension.

"I did the staff schedules," he said, hurrying

to rejoin his interviewer, "told people what to do, supervised the facilities, ordered in any parts we needed, oversaw returns, did the repair budgeting. . . ."

"Real multitasking."

"Sure. You had to have a basic grasp of pretty much every type of industrial activity: construction, painting, electrician's skills, plumbing. . . . But IT, too. I'm an advanced internet user."

"Really?"

"Partly thanks to Asian pornography. I spend a lot of time online looking up Asian pussy."

The audience, whose interest had waned with the discussion of work, seemed to enjoy this remark. In turn, Damián Lobo noted a sparkle in his interlocutor's yellow eyes. It wasn't always easy keeping audience interest at the levels to which O'Kane was accustomed.

"Asian pussy," the presenter repeated.

"It's to do with my fixation with my sister, who's Chinese. Despite the fact we hardly ever see each other. Before today, I hadn't been around to the house in nearly a year. My father hates the smell of cigarettes on my clothes. He always makes this disgusted face when I go to give him a kiss. He's also repulsed by the fact I resemble him physically."

"Are you a heavy smoker?"

"Not really, but the cigarettes I smoke are very aromatic. Camels. I'm going to give up."

"When?"

"At some point. I'll just make the decision, and quit. Once I decide, it won't be hard."

"And you were saying—about being an *advanced* internet user?"

"That's right. Partly because of the thing I mentioned, but also, I've taught courses in programming and data recovery. Partly, as well, because I'm curious by nature and I taught myself how to search the internet without anyone's being able to trace my activities. Quite a lot of my activities took place on the computer at work."

There was a blast of steam from the espresso machine, taking Damián Lobo out of his reverie, and he couldn't be bothered to go back in. Being so popular with audiences always left him feeling a little low.

Calling to the waiter, he paid for the tea and left the café, lighting a cigarette as he stepped outside. He made his way through the streets like a fish at the bottom of the ocean, meandering, weaving in and out, doing anything he could to avoid contact with the other species on the sidewalks.

Soon, he came to a mall with a sign outside for an antiques market that provided aid to a homeless children's charity. He wandered in, hoping to kill a bit of time, in the same way a moray eel might dive into an inviting cave it happened to pass, and found the antiques stalls inside taking up most of the open space within the mall. Had he been managing the building, he thought, there was no way he would have allowed this profusion of booths to block people's access to the emergency exits.

The stalls, which had expensive table linen for awnings—also for sale—displayed a variety of antique clocks, chains, cigarette cases, necklaces, lockets, bracelets, rings. . . . Many of the items were gold and silver and were very old indeed. Damián found it calming even to contemplate such relics.

Suddenly, something on one of the stalls caught his eye. It was a gold tie clip with the initials S.O. engraved on the front.

Sergio O'Kane, Damián thought, smiling to himself. It was small and elegant, with an oval tag with what appeared to be a reference number on it. Perhaps, Damián thought, the price would be on the other side. But he did not dare reach out and turn it over.

Following this curious discovery, he carried on zigzagging through this market in a mall, which felt rather like a high-end bazaar. He was no longer looking very closely at the wares. He couldn't stop thinking about the tie clip.

"What was it that made you think you might be able to steal it?" asked Sergio O'Kane.

"Maybe it was having lost my job," said Damián. "Maybe that just broke me."

"Had you been having financial difficulties, Señor Lobo?"

"No. I'd been given a hefty compensation package, and I still had two years of full welfare support ahead. Plus some savings. But losing your job when you're forty-three years old . . . you can feel pretty low."

"Do you think it would be fair to say that this act of larceny was your way of getting back at the system?"

"Possibly. I also liked the idea of giving you the tie clip as a present, and there is the coincidence that you're among the few people in the world who still use a tie clip. And given that it had your initials engraved on it, I thought, What could be more perfect?"

Pausing the imaginary proceedings, Damián returned to the mall, feeling ready to do whatever it took to get the tie clip. Theft was the method he eventually chose, since when he went back to the stall, there was nobody nearby, and the two apparent stallholders—a pair of predatory old women with teased-up hair—had their backs turned and were arguing over the best place to put a silver-rimmed glass pitcher. Damián Lobo, when pressed by Sergio O'Kane, affirmed that it had all happened very quickly, but at the same time almost in slow motion.

"I felt my hand coming out of my pants pocket, empty, and going back inside it holding the tie clip. It was like a chameleon flicking its tongue out to catch a butterfly."

After the theft, he said, he carried on walking, a neutral look on his face. If the preceding moments had taken place in a dimension where time no longer functioned normally, once he had walked a short distance, the passing seconds began to transpire at their usual pace, although his heart rate rocketed, not unlike that of a person in shock. He felt bad about stealing from the old women, but at the same time his remorse was diminished by a sudden wave of self-consciousness. Walk normally, he had said to himself; don't hurry, don't arouse any suspicions.

He registered something in his peripheral vision now, something not quite right. Turning his head a little to one side, he spotted a security guard trailing him. The man had surely seen the act, and was following at a discreet distance, planning to seize him in a less busy part of the mall. They want to avoid any incidents, Damián thought. Once more, time took on the qualities of a bubble inside which he was trapped, and within which the passing seconds, so malleable, ticked by not in accordance with Damián's morally scrupulous character, but in response to his panic at a possible arrest.

"Imagine me getting caught stealing," he said to Sergio O'Kane. "Think of the people I used to work with, my father, my neighbors, my Chinese sister. . . ."

Damián headed in the direction of one of the busy escalators, hoping the mass of bodies would both impede the security guard and provide himself with cover. But the security guard soon caught up.

"We're going to do this without making a fuss," said the man in uniform, smiling. "I'm going to walk ahead, and you're going to follow me."

"Where are we going?"

"To the office. All routine procedure."

"But I've done nothing wrong."

"Perfect," said the man. "In that case, we'll be done in no time at all."

The security guard moved away from the people standing in line for the escalator, glancing behind him to make sure Damián did as he was told. They passed a perfume store, a gift store, a Japanese food outlet, and a lingerie store, Damián trailing behind, looking at the scenes taking place behind the window displays, as if underwater. They came to a stairwell, and he suddenly bolted down the stairs, gaining a few decisive seconds on the unsuspecting guard.

He flew down the stairs until he came to a metal door, which he barged through. He found himself in a parking lot, which had likewise been taken over by antiques stalls, except that here it was mainly furniture for sale.

As inconspicuously as he could, he found a very large wardrobe and hid behind it. From there, he could see the metal door, and within moments the security guard burst through it. The man came forward, clearly tense but at the same time showing the kind of composure he had doubtless been trained to exercise in such situations. His eyes swept the space as he talked to someone through a mike concealed in his jacket. After a moment, he turned to his left, passing Lobo on his right, who, circling the wardrobe to keep out of the guard's line of sight, came around to the front of the piece of furniture. Glancing around to make sure no one was looking, he opened the middle door and got inside.

2

STANDING IN the dark of the wardrobe, Damián held his breath and listened intently to the activity outside. He thought it very unlikely he would not have been seen getting in; surely it was only a matter of time before somebody ordered him to come out. But seconds passed, then minutes, without his fears being realized. His heart rate returned to normal and his eyes adjusted to the dark, the little light filtering in at the edges of the doors giving him a sense of the spaciousness of his wooden cavern. And, as he had noted before climbing inside, it was indeed an old three-door wardrobe, with a large mirror on the middle door and the panels dividing up the sections removed. With the drawers also taken out, the whole space was see-through—if it's possible to use such a word in almost total darkness.

"The first thing," said Damián to Sergio O'Kane, "was to sit down and think. That's what I used to do in my job anytime something urgent came up—stop and think for a minute. If you react straightaway, you're bound to end up going wrong. Some pipes might drip, but the actual leak is hardly ever in the place where the water's collecting. Water, just like sound waves, seeks the path of least resistance, even if it sometimes doesn't seem the most logical route. The puddle and the leak may be at very opposite ends of the building."

"What was the first thing you worked out, then?" asked O'Kane.

"That I needed to put my cell phone on silent. I don't get very many calls, but if I got one then, it would have been game over."

"And next?"

"Next, I decided just to stay put till I was sure they'd stopped looking for me, and not move a muscle, no matter how worried I got. Like a moray eel in a tiny crevice. It was six in the evening. I figured, worst case, the mall would be shutting at nine."

Still talking to O'Kane, Damián took out his cell phone and switched it to silent mode. Then, activating the screen, which wouldn't be bright enough to be seen through the cracks, he held it up and examined the interior of the wardrobe. He guessed from the exquisite dovetailed corners that the piece was at least a hundred years old.

Made of oak, it seemed very sturdily put together, and he tried to pick out the different smells floating around inside.

"There was a hint of the kind of chemical spray you use for treating woodworm," he told O'Kane. "And holding my cell phone up to one of the side panels, I did see signs of woodworm, their little telltale furrows, though not especially deep. If you treat oak properly, it becomes as hard as steel. My guess was that the partitions and drawers had been taken out due to their having been made of lower-quality wood. You can be damn sure those little wood-boring larvae had had a field day with all of that."

"Go on. . . ."

"Well, in those days, you see, they tended to use oak for the main body of a piece of furniture, and pine, which they didn't have to import, for the incidentals. And with that kind of pine, the woodworm went right through it like butter."

"And what other smells could you detect?"

"Damp, and saltiness. The wardrobe had likely come from some coastal location. That would account for the woodworm, too."

"And what else did it smell of?"

"Old clothes."

"Old clothes? Surely you imagined that."

"Believe me when I tell you, Señor O'Kane, I am blessed with an exceptional sense of smell. That wardrobe had been home to generations of suits, and blouses, and underwear—not all as clean as was perhaps proper. Have you heard the thing about stables?"

"I have not."

"The smell of muck lingers on, decades after the horses and everything else have been cleared out. Ask anyone who lives in a historic part of any town or city."

Without breaking off from the TV interview (which, O'Kane now announced to one of the cameras, was currently a global "trending topic"), Damián checked the time and took stock. He had been inside the wardrobe for an hour now. Clearly, no one had seen him get in, but there was nothing to say they wouldn't see him getting out.

He gave it ten minutes (to coincide with the latest commercial break) before resolving to open one of the side doors a fraction, with the greatest of care. The sight of a security guard's cap was the first thing to greet him. He shut the door and sat back down.

"Were you afraid, Señor Lobo?" asked O'Kane when the final commercial came to an end.

"Very," said Damián. "I felt so ashamed. I'd rather have died than been found out."

"And what of the tie clip?"

"I'd put it in one of my jacket pockets, here, the right-hand one. Every now and then I'd take it out and run my fingers over it, all the while listening to people's conversations outside, and constantly poised in case a prospective buyer should happen to open one of the doors."

"What would you have done if they had?"

"Conceal myself at the opposite end to which-ever door it was. I rehearsed the moves I would need to make if that came to pass."

"And did anything, in fact, come to pass?"

"Oh, yes. I must have been in there for a couple of hours, when suddenly one of the doors opened, on the far side from where I was. Light came flood-ing in, like water through a crack in a dam, but it only lit up half of the interior, as though some invisible dike were holding it back. Then a young boy's face appeared. He was eight or ten or twelve years old. I can't say exactly—I don't have kids of my own; I can never work it out. He was outside in the light, so immediately I got a clear view of his face, whereas he must have been barely able to see me in the dark, as I tried to make myself as small and inconspicuous as I could at the opposite end of the wardrobe. But see *something* he did, and he stood looking straight at me, until, a few fractions of a second later, I saw panic on his face—his eyes had obviously adjusted and he could fully see me now. I put my finger to my lips: *Shhh.* He backed away, and I then heard his mother telling him to stop touching things."

"And?"

"And nothing. Luckily, the boy didn't say a word, though he did fail to shut the door, so I spent the next minute or two panicking, until somebody came by and shut it from the outside."

"Have you thought about the boy at all since?" asked O'Kane.

"A great deal. How would that moment play out in his later life? I've wondered about that."

"How do you think it will play out?"

"I don't know for sure. Inexplicable things always happen to us when we're kids, things we never tell anyone about. We grow up, and we put it all behind us."

"Did any such things happen to you?"

"Well, there was one time, I must have been six or seven, and I opened the oven door, to find the head of a camel inside, staring straight back at me with its eyes wide open."

This drew laughter from O'Kane and the audience.

"And why did you come to be opening that oven door?"

"Well, the oven was broken, it wasn't being used by anyone, and for a while I'd been hiding bits of fudge inside it, little marzipan figurines as well, things I'd taken from the pantry. I wanted to have my own supplies ready when Christmas came."

"It sounds as though you were quite light-fingered from an early age." O'Kane scratched his chin.

"No, no, I mean . . ." Damián was wrong-footed. "I never really thought of that as stealing. Just something kids do, wouldn't you say?"

"And did you go back to the oven to retrieve your sweets?"

"Never. They became all maggoty, and there were arguments in the house for weeks afterward, months even, since nobody could understand how they had gotten there or why they had been abandoned like that."

3

I T WAS NEARLY closing time—for which Damián had decided to wait before attempting his escape—when he felt the wardrobe suddenly lift and tilt, as if it were being picked up. It was being picked up. As it swayed and shook, Damián heard the workmen discussing different strategies for transporting it.

"Let me put some tape across the doors," said one. "They aren't locked; they're gonna fly open and hit us in the face."

"But why the hell don't we take it apart, then move it?" said another. "The proper way."

"Because it's over a hundred years old," said a third man, "and it wasn't built so you could take it apart. You have to shift it in one piece."

"Christ! Feels like there's a dead body in there."

"It's solid oak, that's why. How they used to make things."

Damián heard the sound of the packing tape and decided to lie down to distribute his weight more evenly, and thereby avoid suspicion that any-thing, or anyone, was inside. Luckily, he was a thin man, and not that tall, either, and he guessed they would think his weight was just part and parcel of the massive wardrobe. He lay there as the work-men lifted it up and carried it to what he imagined was the bed of a truck, to a confused sound track of groans, signals, and orders.

A pause followed while they battened the wardrobe down, he assumed, before the truck set off. This should have been an opportune moment to get out, so if the truck stopped at a red light, or even just slowed down, he would be ready to jump off and make his getaway. But it immediately became apparent to him that at least two of the workmen were traveling in the bed of the truck as well, possibly because there wasn't enough space up front, possibly to make sure the wardrobe didn't slide around.

"They were having a conversation about seda-tives," Damián said to O'Kane.

"Sedatives? Are you sure?"

The audience laughed. There was a smattering of applause as well, but O'Kane motioned for them to be quiet; he wished to keep things moving. His interviewee then described moving from one end of the wardrobe to the other, putting an ear to one of the side panels, then to the opposite one, to follow the conversation. A picture that sent the audience into fits of laughter once again.

Given that Damián's real-life escapade and the TV interview were going on simultaneously, he had to flit back and forth between them at breakneck speed, on top of which he had the jolting of the vehicle and the roar of the traffic to contend with, because though the truck bed was enclosed, the outside noise filtered in through its edges.

"The roof must have been made of tarpaulin," Damián explained, "because you could hear the wind ruffling it, like the sound of an awning."

"But what were the men saying about sedatives?"

"One of them said that ever since he'd started taking sedatives, the world had still been in him, but he was no longer in the world. To which the other guy said, if he ever found a way to escape the world, he wouldn't be coming back in a hurry, least of all to get a job in removals."

Quiet descended over the TV studio, intentionally prolonged by O'Kane, a master of timing, to add suspense.

"Did anything else happen?"

"Well," Damián added reluctantly, "one of them was telling a joke about vocal chords."

O'Kane had recently undergone a minor

operation to remove some polyps on his own vocal chords, so his interest was piqued. But Damián was still hesitant.

"It's in pretty bad taste," he said.

Far from deterring O'Kane, and indeed the audience, their interest swelled.

"Really, I wish I hadn't mentioned it. It honestly isn't the kind of thing you want to hear on TV."

"Come on now, don't make us beg," said O'Kane, backed by enthusiastic applause from the audience.

"Okay, so a man goes to the doctor and says, 'I've got a problem with my fecal chords.' 'Vocal cords, you mean,' said the doctor. 'No,' said the man, 'I have no problem going to the bathroom, it's just that every time I open my mouth, I start talking shit.'"

Sergio O'Kane burst out laughing, and the audience hooted and clapped along. It was time for a quick commercial break, and Damián took the opportunity to appraise his real-world situation, to which there had been no discernible improvement. The truck had been driving for half an hour. It had long since left downtown, made its way up what seemed to be a freeway, possibly one of the belt-ways, and after that spent a few minutes in traffic before joining what he sensed was another freeway. Damián had begun to wonder if it was ever going to end; he needed a bathroom, and a cigarette.

He had entered the mall at around six, and his digital watch told him it was now quarter to nine. Three hours in that most absurd of situations, the denouement of which, ecstatic or disastrous, he was constantly trying to imagine.

"Did it not occur to you to get rid of the tie clip, the evidence of your crime?" asked O'Kane when they came back from the commercial break.

"Very much so, but I wanted to give it to you as a present. There was also the fact it had started taking on magical powers. While I still had it, I felt like nothing bad could happen to me."

"But something bad *was* happening to you."

"Nothing worse than what was already happening, I mean."

Just then, the truck came to a halt. From the movements and the noises outside, he guessed they had reached their destination, and he paused the interview accordingly; he would need to concentrate if he were to have any chance of making his getaway. He heard the cab doors open and shut, footsteps on the metal floor of the truck bed, and the workmen begin discussing where and how best to position themselves to maneuver the wardrobe out.

"I had to lie down again," said Damián, taking

himself back to the TV studio, "to spread my weight equally, like before."

"And did you get thrown around as they lifted it off?" asked O'Kane.

"No, luckily, because just then another voice came in, a woman's, and she started shouting at the men to be careful with it. I imagined this must be the person who had bought the wardrobe, and we were at her home."

"You're going to tell me they walked you straight into a private residence?"

"Not yet. The wardrobe was so big, they had to take the frame off the front door of the house, a detached house on the outskirts of the city, from what I could tell; it was dark by now, and I only had the crack between two of the doors to look out through. They also had to take the feet off the wardrobe, and some kind of ornamental molding that was sticking out."

"And during all of that, there wasn't a moment when you could have jumped out and run off?"

"No. There were people there the entire time, and the doors were still taped shut. I thought the tape was bound to make a big noise if I opened the doors. I heard one of the workmen ask the woman what she wanted such an old piece of furniture for, when she was living in a completely modern house, and one, furthermore, that had built-in wardrobes. It had belonged to her grandparents, she said, and had been a feature of a house where she had spent part of her childhood. She'd recognized it at the market, she said, because of a series of little nicks on one side to mark the children's heights as they grew up."

"'Just here,' she said to the man, 'where it says *Lucía*. That's me. And these lines are how tall I was, from the ages of five to ten, which was when I lived with my grandparents.'

"'And these ones,' said the man. 'What's that—*Jorge*?'

"'Exactly,' she said. 'Jorge was my brother. We were the same age, twins, but he died two years after we moved in with my grandparents. Tetanus. That's why the head heights for him stop there.'

"'Jesus,' said the man.

"'When I saw it, I couldn't believe it. I thought I was going to faint. Goodness knows where this poor wardrobe's been in the interim. Here, there, and everywhere. . . .'

"'Like everything in life,' said the man."

4

WITH CONSIDERABLE difficulty, and much groaning and swearing, the wardrobe was carried into the house, at which point the workmen's labors were still not complete; they had to maneuver it into one of the bedrooms, under directions from the woman. Once it was where she wanted it, one or some of the workmen, as far as Damián could tell, set about refitting the bedroom door frame, which had also needed to be removed, and screwing the feet and ornamental molding back onto the wardrobe, while the rest of the team went off to replace the front door frame. The wardrobe was moved up against the wall indicated by the woman, after which the voices went away.

"So now," Damián said to O'Kane, "I pushed on one of the doors, taking the utmost care, and the packing tape, only a few inches of which had been stuck on, came away quite easily. The coast was clear, and I stepped out, feeling dizzy, and nearly tripped over myself, like when you get down off a fairground ride."

"And where had the workmen all gone?" asked the interviewer.

"They'd gathered in the hall with the woman. She'd given them each a beer, and possibly some money, for their pains."

"I get it. And you, I imagine, looked around to get your bearings a little. So tell us, what did you see?"

"I was in the master bedroom, which was pretty spacious and had an en suite bathroom, where I dashed to relieve my bladder. I was bursting. Instead of using the toilet itself, which would have meant flushing and thereby announcing my presence, I used the sink, running the tap afterward. That was how I was thinking, moment by moment, on the fly. I'd never had to think so fast in my life, not even in the stickiest of situations at work, which over the course of twenty-five years were pretty numerous."

The audience began laughing and applauding, while O'Kane gave a wry look and Damián did his best nonplussed expression.

"And I imagine," said O'Kane, once order had been restored, "thinking fast was quite crucial, given the situation."

"Right. The weird thing, though, is that when you're in extreme situations, you're actually still thinking, thinking all the time."

"Thinking what?"

"How I'd explain myself if I was found out. I planned to say I'd been at the antiques market when I started to feel ill and, not knowing what to do, on the brink of passing out, I came upon the wardrobe and just climbed inside. And then I fell asleep. I assumed we'd reached a point where nobody would be making a link between the disappearance of the tie clip and my presence in that house. I doubted anyone had even reported the theft. It was hardly worth much, right? And, worst case, they'd call the police, and I'd tell them the same story. That was what I did while I peed: rehearse, word for word, the alibi I'd have to sell to the woman, and to the police if it came to that."

"But it never did."

"No, because when I finished peeing, the woman was still with the workmen. That meant I couldn't make for the front door myself, because they'd see me. In fact, when I poked my head out of the room, it looked like all escape routes were blocked. My only option was to go farther inside the house, though that didn't seem likely to help my cause very much."

And that was what Damián did. After a few moments' hesitation, and hearing the woman bid the workmen good-bye and step back inside the house, he dived under the bed, assuming she would be coming to open the wardrobe in order to bask in its immense proportions.

And indeed, the woman came in and tore off all the packing tape, opened each of the doors to let in a little air, and stuck her head inside the wardrobe. She inhaled deeply, like someone leaning out over an abyss.

"Then," Lobo said to O'Kane, "she proceeded to take some clothes from a pile on the bed and put them on hangers in the wardrobe."

"And you, right there, looking up from under the bed."

"Yes, I had a view of her bare feet, since she'd taken her shoes off, and part of her legs, up as far as a billowing skirt. She went back and forth between bed and wardrobe, singing contentedly to herself. Now I'll tell you something you'll find surprising."

"Go on."

"After all those hours inside the wardrobe, that spot beneath the bed seemed positively comfy by comparison."

The audience laughed and clapped, while Damián looked out impassively. O'Kane gave the cameras a look somewhere between complicity and irony.

"*Comfy*?" he said. "Truly?"

"Yes, truly. All I needed now was a cigarette and my happiness would have been complete. The carpet was extremely thick, so I wasn't cold at all. There was enough clear space between me and the bed slats that I didn't feel cramped, but they weren't so high off the ground that I was going to be seen. Plus, the bedspread hung down a little way. No way she was going to be sticking her head in there for a look, not unless she was crazy. Or, okay, unless she was vacuuming."

"And what about you," said O'Kane, "are you the kind of crazy person who goes around checking beneath beds before you go to sleep?"

"Well actually, yes," Damián conceded with a smile. "But I think I'm in the minority. People just reconcile themselves to that metaphysical space beneath their bodies."

Sergio O'Kane turned to the audience, whose ebullience it was necessary to quell from time to time if the interview was to avoid disintegrating completely, and asked for a show of hands: Who there checked under his or her bed at night? Less than a third of them put their hands up. A few hands were half-raised, as if people were ashamed to admit it, or as if they couldn't decide whether to tell the truth or miss out on the chance to be on camera.

"So," said O'Kane, "there you were, in that—what did you call it? A metaphysical space?"

"That's a way of suggesting its complexity. My father often said it. In his view, Hitchcock's films were that kind of frightening."

"So, in a space that you checked every single night . . ."

"Weird, right? Like someone falling into the abyss he's been leaning over."

Just then, a voice was heard elsewhere in the house, calling "Hello!" as the front door slammed shut. Damián Lobo departed from the TV studio and put his whole being on high alert.

The woman called back: "Come up here, Fede, quick! I've got a surprise."

Within moments, a man appeared in the bedroom.

"Look," said the woman, "my grandparents' wardrobe, it's finally arrived."

The man came forward, kissed the woman—doubtless his wife—and feigned enthusiasm, which he then went on to undermine by enumerating the downsides of this new addition. First was the fact it was standing directly in front of a built-in wardrobe, now rendered useless. His wife said they'd talked this through already, and it was the only possible place.

"It's absurd to have that dead space behind it," he protested. "It's like a kind of gulag."

"The one thing we've got more than enough of in this house is space," she said.

The husband also pointed out the lack of drawers.

"Where are we supposed to put our underwear?" he asked.

This they had also discussed before, she said, and she had put their underwear in the wardrobe in the guest room. It was clear to Damián that the conversation was subtly turning fraught, however much the wife, Lucía, was trying to keep calm. Eventually, she protested that her husband was spoiling the moment.

"Don't you see?" she said. "My brother and I used to hide inside this wardrobe when we were little; it was our den. It's . . . the one thing I have to remember him by."

"Slightly creepy memory, if you ask me," said the man called Fede.

Now a third person entered the room, a teenage girl, from what Damián could tell, the couple's daughter, either having recently arrived home or having been in another of the rooms while the workmen brought the wardrobe in. The girl was evidently startled by the piece of furniture.

"It's like something out of a movie!" she cried.

"A horror movie," said the father.

"I feel like everyone but me's allowed to have things they like!" cried Lucía. "Everyone but me!"

"Now the husband," said Damián to O'Kane, "could obviously tell she was at her breaking point, and he started to backpedal."

"And the daughter?" asked O'Kane.

"She wasn't really against it, I don't think. In some subtle way, I'd say she was on her mother's side, while at the same time not seeming to want to contradict her father directly."

"So what happened next?"

"The three of them left the room to go eat their supper."

"And what did you do?" asked O'Kane.

"I stayed where I was, all alone under the bed."

5

WHEN THE COUPLE got into bed that night, the husband made one or two amorous attempts, but she, possibly still upset over his earlier criticisms, made it clear his attentions were not welcome. The husband turned over in the bed, switched on a radio on his bedside table, and, like water from a tap, the voices of a sports show came gushing out. She snapped at him to turn it off, and he did as he was told, the noise ending as abruptly as it had begun.

In the meantime, Damián went into deep contemplation of the woman sleeping, or trying to sleep, barely six inches from where he lay. Though he had not seen her face, he felt captivated by her voice, which was thick, throaty, as though wrapped up in gauze. He shut his eyes and remembered the sight of her bare feet, with toes that had struck him as abnormally long but nonetheless so shapely that they wouldn't have looked out of place on a small hand. He tried picturing her as she climbed between the sheets, and whether she would have been wearing pajamas or a camisole, or perhaps was naked. Never had he been in a situation of such intimacy with a woman who was not Chinese (or at least so he believed), and he began to grow excited. He considered telling Sergio O'Kane about it, and while he tried to decide whether to or not, he reached down, unzipped his trousers, and started fondling himself. He barely realized he was masturbating until it was nearly over; his movements had become altogether ghostly, and the way he touched himself could even have brought relief to a dead man.

He felt despondent when it was over. He imagined being back on O'Kane's show, recounting the sordid details in front of the studio audience and the millions of viewers at home. People would find it hilarious; they loved this kind of thing on television; it would be a hit. But, he asked himself, what about his dignity? Was it worth sacrificing his dignity on the altar of viewer ratings? Yes, he decided, it was. After all, O'Kane's show existed in a world completely disconnected from this one. But it also struck him he'd be better off saving the story for one of those moments when, for reasons that aren't entirely clear, the people watching at home felt an impulse to switch channels.

Nonetheless, perhaps out of a postejaculatory fragility, he returned to the imaginary TV studio and confessed to O'Kane that he had never been with a Western woman in his life. Or any woman, in fact, apart from his Chinese sister.

A respectful hush descended over the audience. His yellow-eyed interviewer also said nothing for a few moments, until he asked, "Would you rather we didn't poke around too much on this subject?"

"Yes," said Damián. "I'd much rather that."

"But I suppose one of the things to be said is that you have lived a solitary life."

"Fairly. Since I left home, which was a long time ago now, I've seen my sister only rarely, though she's always been a part of my sexual fantasies. Plus, my job was conducive to the kind of self-isolation I had a natural propensity for. My desk was in the basement of the building. There, among old metal shelving units piled high with moldy box files, themselves overflowing with documents no one ever looked at, I had a hovel of a workshop, which I shared for a while with my manager, an elderly guy, very handy but incredibly withdrawn, more like he'd gone inside a prison cell than merely retreated into his shell. It was an old, old building, and there would be hours when the sound of the pipes, all the echoing drips and gurgles, was my only company. I kept up a conversation in my head with the noises. I imagined them telling me things, silly things, nothing of import, and me responding, again just little quips and asides, stuff about my day. The phone sometimes rang, and we'd have to go up to one of the offices to do a repair: a drawer that wasn't closing properly, a flickering strip light, a door that had come off its hinges, a broken lock. . . . We unblocked the toilets, did checks on the elevator, bled the radiators, kept the old AC units clear. . . . This was all before the days of planned obsolescence. Do you know what that is?"

"Yes," said O'Kane. "I saw the documentary."

"In a world where things tend to be replaced rather than repaired, there's no call for either my manual skills or my technical know-how. After my manager died, which was pretty soon after I started the job, it was just me in the basement, talking to the ambient noises, feeding the mice, which inhabited the building in their hundreds, and surfing the net—I've already told you what for. There were always things that needed fixing, sure, but times changed, and a lot of the maintenance work started getting outsourced. They used a company owned by the boss's nephew, and I became the go-between. That was when I had contact with all the young engineers. Then, little by little, in part because of the way things were going and in part because I started making myself less available, people at the company started skipping me and going directly to the boss's nephew. I only did odd jobs, less and less crucial to the actual running of the building, and less and less frequent. My last two years were spent almost entirely down in the basement, with only the computer for company; I came to know it better than I did the inside of my own head. A point came when I thought I'd been forgotten about entirely, and that perhaps it was going to go on that way forever. That was when the redundancy notice appeared in my pigeonhole."

"You are a very honest person," said O'Kane.

"That's what comes of feeling like shit," said Damián. "Feeling like shit makes you honest."

"And tell me, did it take them long to get to sleep, the couple whose bed you were lying under?"

"No, I don't know, really—the normal amount of time. He snored a bit. She wasn't a snorer, but if you listened closely to her breathing, you could tell she was asleep."

Damián felt his cell phone vibrate in his pocket. Someone had sent him a text message, and he opened it while shielding the screen to prevent the light from spilling out into the room. It was from the bank. Apparently, he had been entered in a contest to win a Samsung tablet, and he needed to follow a link to find out if he had won. When, returning to the interview, he recounted this, the audience clapped and laughed.

"Just then," said Damián, "I really wasn't so dissimilar to a moray eel hiding in a crevice in the coral."

"And what about your getaway? Wasn't this your moment?"

"I wasn't really thinking about that. Although I wasn't thinking about sleeping, either. I was just lying there, not really aware I was just lying there. I just let the minutes pass, feeling the weight of the tie clip as I turned it over in my hands."

"The tie clip!" said O'Kane. "I'd forgotten about that! The tie clip was how this whole thing started, and you still haven't shown it to us."

Damián held the tie clip out to the presenter, but it remained in his hand, underlining the inherent lack of connection between the two realities he inhabited. O'Kane took an imaginary version of the object from him and held it up to one of the cameras, so people could see the engraving of his initials. The audience clapped. Then Sergio O'Kane turned to Damián Lobo once again.

"What happened next?" he asked.

"I fell into a jumpy kind of sleep, or a drowsy vigilance, all my senses simultaneously switched off and on high alert. Kind of how I imagine soldiers slept in the trenches."

6

AT QUARTER TO SEVEN, the radio on the bedside table came on, which it had been programmed to do in lieu of an alarm. A segment of local news was playing. A truck carrying pigs as livestock had turned over on the M-40, at the exit for Valencia, littering the freeway with dozens of animal carcasses. Motorists were being advised to find alternative routes. The bed slats shook and creaked with the movements of the husband and wife as they stretched and surrendered themselves to wakefulness. A light came on—it was still dark outside—and Damián turned to watch whatever he could of these people's lives through the gap between bedspread and floor.

A rapid coming and going of feet ensued, first in the environs of the bed, then between bedroom and bathroom. The movements gave the impression of a well-drilled sequence. With a kind of methodicalness, the shower ran for a short while, the cistern emptied and filled up again, and there came the discreet hum of a shaver, followed by the electrical urgency of a hair dryer. Damián felt a few faint drafts as the doors to the antique wardrobe were opened and closed.

"Rather than just listening to this reality," he said to O'Kane in a fleeting escape to the show, "I put a stethoscope up to its beating heart; I had to be alive to the tiniest danger signal."

"And was there any?"

"Well, yes. At one point the wife, Lucía, asked the husband if he'd taken up smoking again. 'Why?' he said. 'I don't know,' she replied, 'I've caught a few whiffs of smoke. I'm worried María's smoking in secret.'"

"It was you she could smell," said O'Kane.

"My clothes. You know the way cigarette smoke lingers. Luckily, the parents stuck with the idea of its being the daughter, whose name I found out was María. Lucía, María, and Fede—for Federico, I guess. No fancy names, a normal family."

The couple left the bedroom and then came back in several times, passing by the guest room, Damián supposed, to get some of the underwear they hadn't been able to put in the antique wardrobe due to its lack of drawers. They took turns banging on the daughter's door as they passed, shouting at her to get up. At certain points, each came and sat on the bed, keeping to their respective sides, and showing their bare heels to Damián, who was thereby able to prolong his appreciation of the wife's feet. The coordination of movements led him to surmise that the trio would leave together, before going their separate ways.

Their activities moved to another part of the house—the kitchen, by the sounds Damián now began to hear: the clatter of cups and cutlery mingled with talk. But the words came apart as they traveled down the corridor, and by the time they had reached Damián's eardrums, they were the mere fragments of what had once been a practical conversation.

After a short while, the woman came back into the bedroom. She was wearing a pair of black heels with pointed toes. The man came in soon after, in brown shoes and beige pinstriped trousers. She asked him to shut the window, which one of the two had opened earlier to air out the room.

"And please remember," she said, "while we haven't got any help, you can't just leave your things lying around like you normally do."

Included in these things were a pair of socks and some boxer shorts, which lay on the floor just at the edge of Damián's hiding place. A shadow slid nearer, and he held his breath, just as the man's hand appeared in his field of vision, gathering the dirty garments and immediately disappearing.

After that, the trio made their way to the same point in the hall; there came the sound of a door opening and shutting—the one joining house and garage, thought Damián. Now it was just him. And yet, feeling that one couldn't be too careful, he decided to stay put for a further half hour, in case any of the family had forgotten something and suddenly reappeared.

Though he had heard none of those courtesy beeps given off by house alarms to tell the owners how long they've got to clear the perimeter, he decided to proceed as though a home security system had indeed been activated. Peeking out from under the bed, he scanned the four or five possible spots where CCTV cameras might be placed, but he saw none. He maneuvered himself slowly into the open, and stood up, also slowly, alert to the possibility of a motion detector going off. None did.

"And weren't you feeling a bit stiff?" asked O'Kane.

"A little, yes. But I didn't notice at first. The body, in situations as tense as that, disappears."

"Right. So what next?"

"First I went to the bathroom to relieve myself. Then I walked out of the bedroom and along the hall, making absolutely sure there weren't any alarms elsewhere in the house, either. It turned out to be a three-bedroom bungalow, the rooms distributed in a fairly standard way. The kitchen/ living room was at one end of the house, with a breakfast bar across the space between them. The hall led from the front of the house back to the bedrooms (or vice versa). The daughter's bedroom and a separate bathroom were on one side, and on the other the master bedroom with its en suite bath, and the guest room. The hall ended (or began) just inside the front door, with a reception space with a large closet and a lavatory on one side. Out front, there was a small garden, a driveway leading into the garage, and out back was a larger garden, accessed by doors leading off both the kitchen and living room. Grassy passageways ran along either side of the house, connecting front and back gardens. Though I looked out of the windows—taking care not to be seen—I had no idea which part of Madrid I'd ended up in."

"But on the outskirts, evidently," said O'Kane.

"Yes. All the nearby properties were identical bungalows. Some kind of housing development in the suburbs."

"Now it was time to get out of there."

"On an objective level, yes, it was. But instead, I

went to the kitchen, because I was hungry. Remember, I hadn't eaten anything since the previous day. I put some milk in a cup and heated it up in the microwave, and then I found some madeleines to dunk. As I broke my fast, I did a few stretches; now that things had calmed down, I started to feel the effects of my night beneath the bed."

"Okay, so you did some stretches, limbering up. Then what?"

"I decided not to smoke the first cigarette of the day. Or the second one. I actually took the pack out of my jacket, removed all the cigarettes, and threw them down the toilet. I flushed several times, until every last scrap had gone, every filter and shred of tobacco. The pack itself I burned in the kitchen sink, washing the ashes down the drain. And there you have it: I gave up smoking."

"No acupuncture, no nicotine patches," said O'Kane in a sardonic tone, to the audience's delight.

"And since the sink was full of dirty dishes," continued Damián, "both from breakfast and from the previous night's dinner, I took my jacket off, rolled up my sleeves, and did the washing-up."

The studio audience burst into laughter, while O'Kane gave the camera one of his trademark conspiratorial smiles, the kind that had brought him such success over the course of his career. In

close-up, there was something troublingly hyp-
notic about the yellow of his eyes, an effect he
accentuated by arching now one eyebrow, now
the other.

"So," he said mischievously, "you washed the
dishes."

"Yes. They had a dishwasher, but I've always
liked doing the washing-up. There's something
very Zen about it. You stand there at the sink, and
your thoughts just float around, with no apparent
design. But then you start to see that in fact your
thoughts have been working together, interweaving, turning into something, though you can't say
what precisely. I've sometimes found that, looking into a sparkling, freshly rinsed cup, my mind
is suddenly completely blank, clean, empty—just
like the cup in my hands. And it's then—how to put
it?—it's then that you get a fleeting sense of what it
means to be at one with everything."

"Would you call yourself religious?"

"Not religious precisely, not in the generally
accepted meaning of the word anyway. Thinking
of the cup, I'm reminded of a documentary I saw
on TV where they talked about Japanese bowls."

"For rice? That kind of bowl?"

"That kind. The simplicity of a rice bowl

conceals a remarkable degree of complexity. It's as though each bowl contains a universe inside it."

"So there's a kind of ecstasy for you in the washing of dishes?"

"Not ecstasy, no, but a feeling of being at peace with myself, something totally lacking since I lost my job. It was being unemployed that had pushed me to commit an act like stealing the tie clip—the kind of thing someone like me would never have done before, I can assure you. I wasn't myself, and I could now see that *that* was why I had done such a thing. Everything was in flux; I was frightened—frightened of the future. Fear is one of the most pernicious feelings possible. It has the power to transform you, to turn you into the worst kind of lowlife. And I had been afraid. I'd stolen out of fear, and fear had prompted all that followed, this strange sequence of events. But here's the thing: I'm there, I'm doing the dishes, I've got one of the family's cups in my hand—the daughter's, I guessed, from the dregs of hot chocolate in the bottom—when suddenly this feeling of peace comes over me. And this peacefulness, whether or not you believe me, stemmed from the cup, from its concave bottom. The cup was at peace, and that peace was transmitted to me, a kind of peace that left no space for fear."

A hush had settled on the imaginary studio audience. People held their breath, hanging on Damián's every word. Sergio O'Kane had a message in his earpiece from production, saying there had been a sudden spike in viewers tuning in. "Keep him on this," said the director.

"What you are describing," O'Kane said, "is a mystical experience."

"A mystical experience?" Damián replied, apparently reluctant to take this idea seriously. "No, that's too much. All I'm saying is, the fear had gone. And there is no freedom like the absence of fear."

"And tell us, what was the upshot?"

"Well, after tidying up the kitchen, I walked around the house. There were lots of family photos in the living room, so I got to see what they all looked like, and the mother, sure enough, wasn't Chinese. Or the daughter. Neither Chinese nor adopted, because I found a folder in one of the drawers with all their documents and certificates, and there was nothing amiss. But the curious thing is, though none of them were Chinese, I found it very pleasant to look at their faces—especially the mother's. It was the first time I've felt like that about a Western woman."

"So you were attracted to her?"

"I don't know if *attracted* is the right word

exactly—possibly, though. It was like something in her might free me from my Asian fixation. I've read about sexual fixations on the internet. Some people are born with a certain fixation, but by the end of their lives they wind up with a different one. I'm obviously talking about serious, serious fixations."

"Like your fixation with your sister."

"Like my fixation with my sister."

"So what else did you deduce from the family photos?"

"Well, they were a young family. The parents were somewhere in their forties and the daughter, as I'd guessed, was fourteen or fifteen. The furniture was all new, all Ikea things, which led me to think they hadn't lived in the house for long, maybe a year or so. One of the photos of the mother had been taken from such an angle that her eyes followed me around the room, wherever I went. You know how certain pictures can do that."

"Of course," said O'Kane.

"She just kept on looking at me, whether I went and stood over to the right or over to the left, whether I crouched down or stood up on a chair. I went and hid behind the door, for example, and slowly, slowly leaned my head around it, trying to catch her off guard, but the moment I looked at her—or before, possibly—she was already looking at me. But now I didn't feel like she was watching me in a guarded way; rather, it seemed that she was looking at me pleadingly, as though she was asking for my help."

"And what was her face like?"

"It was like her voice."

A pause now followed, with Damián Lobo feeling he had answered the question, and Sergio O'Kane waiting for him to go on. Eventually, O'Kane broke the silence.

"And what was her voice like?"

"Slightly muffled, I'd say, like it was wrapped in gauze."

"And to look at? Could you describe her?"

"The same, like a woman emerging out of the mist, or at the end of a long sickness, a convalescent with a startled look, mouth agape, as though she needed to take in more air than she could through her nostrils alone. She had small eyes, and a small nose—very small, I'd say. Deficient somehow, or childish, though not in an ungenerous way. You couldn't see her ears, as she hid them behind a shoulder-length bob."

"Did she seem attractive to you?"

"Not in the normal way."

"And what about him?"

"He was good-looking, in a tennis player sort of

way. I'm not saying he necessarily played tennis—I don't know about that—but there was an ease both in his looks and in his body, like that of a tennis player. He was attractive in a conventional, standard sort of way; you know the type: square jaw, large mouth, wide-set eyes, one of those flat faces with a pug nose."

"You paint a very clear picture," said O'Kane.

"Thank you, Sergio. The daughter was very thin, she looked a bit small to me for her age, and otherwise resembled her mother."

"So tell us, what else did you do, apart from looking at the photographs?"

"I fixed one of the cupboard doors in the kitchen. The unit was new, but the door hadn't been hung properly."

"The hinges on those cupboards are such a headache."

"Sure, if you don't understand them. Most people don't. They're called 'cabinet hinges.' There are a lot of videos on YouTube about how to assemble them. All this one needed was a couple of screws tightened. I used one of the pointed-end kitchen knives—it's got Phillips screws, as you know."

These comments were interspersed with laughter from the audience, and O'Kane appeared happy with the proceedings, as though the news via his earpiece was good.

"So," he said now, cutting in, "you did the washing-up, you fixed the door on the kitchen cupboard. . . ."

"I made the beds, too, the daughter's and the one in the master bedroom; all they'd done was to throw the sheets and the covers back on any old way, and flung the bedspreads over to make it look like a good job. I stood in the daughter's room for a few minutes, hardly looking through her things at all. I somehow couldn't bring myself to go rummaging around in her stuff."

"I understand."

"I'd already straightened the whole place up a bit, and it was still pretty early, so I went and turned on the TV in the living room. I'd never watched TV at that time of day. The mere idea of it depressed me, like having a drink at breakfast. I soon turned the TV off again, and then, going out into the hall, I noticed a trapdoor with one of those cords hanging from it, the kind you pull and a ladder drops down. I pulled it, the ladder opened out, and I climbed up. There was a tiny attic space, too low to stand up in, even in the middle. A miniloft, you might call it, stuffed with all manner of things—a couple of sets of luggage, a wicker trunk full of old toys and teddy bears, a cradle, a high chair. There were cardboard boxes, held together with tape, and an old TV set next to a pile of VHS cassettes—they're historical artifacts now—plus a couple of video players. And a collection of children's books, magazines, and a few piles of well-thumbed books about ghosts and the paranormal in general. I found another wicker trunk, this one full of men's clothing, the kind of things people stop wearing but can't bring themselves to throw away. There was a tracksuit, in a fabric that was nice and cozy, which was almost exactly my size. The women's clothing, however, had been hung from a portable rack on wheels, with a dust sheet over the top. I took the tracksuit, climbed back down, and shut the trap door. Then I went into the master bedroom, placed the tracksuit on the bed, and had a look at the wardrobe for the marks the woman had talked about. And there they were, on the right-hand side. Her name, Lucía, had been scratched into the wood next to the horizontal marks for her heights over the years, ages five to ten. Next to that was her brother's name, Jorge, his marks coming to a stop where it said age seven. As I looked, I allowed an idea to grow in my mind, something that had begun without my knowing it, almost behind my back . . . something I still wasn't sure if I'd be able to pull off."

"Would you be happy to share?" asked O'Kane.

"I emptied everything out of the old wardrobe, laying the clothes on the bed so I'd be able to hang them up again in the correct order. I couldn't help but take in the scent of some of Lucía's clothes, though I was careful not to take any pleasure in that—even just touching her things struck me as slightly perverted. Anyway, I proceeded as respectfully as I could. Once everything was out, I took a look at the back of the wardrobe, which, I had rightly remembered, was comprised of three panels separated by decorative beading. By my calculations, the middle panel lined up more or less exactly with the middle of the built-in wardrobe, which, of course, you couldn't access now. I was more or less beside myself by this point."

"Beside yourself?" asked O'Kane.

"I dashed out to the garage, where, as expected, I found a toolbox. I took it back through with me to the bedroom and then pulled the antique wardrobe out, away from the built-in one behind. I took the doors off the built-in wardrobe and placed them inside—it went quite a long way back—over the drawers that ran the whole length of the space, forming a kind of top. I then pulled the middle panel off the back of the antique wardrobe, without damaging it as such, and used the hinges from the door of the built-in wardrobe to turn the panel into a hidden door; the decorative beading helped disguise the joins. I pushed the antique wardrobe back into position and then climbed inside it to make sure it was possible to access the space behind. It was, and when I shut my improvised middle door, I found it was indeed impossible to tell the difference. I could hardly contain myself—I mean, you can imagine—so I took the toolbox back to the garage, quickly went up to the attic and found some old sheets, plus an old washbasin, which I took back to the bedroom. I laid the sheets over the doors I'd put inside the built-in wardrobe, then lay down on them to see if the fit was good. There was still space for the washbasin, which I didn't really plan on using unless it was an absolute emergency. To sum up, while the family was at home, I'd be able to live in there, in the space that the man, Fede, had called a kind of gulag. There was even light if I needed it, with a bulb that came on automatically when you opened the doors. With the doors removed, you could still turn the bulb on or off by just tightening or loosening it. To do this, I had to leave it uncovered, as it was protected by a decorative plastic cap held in place by a couple of screws."

"Like being inside a coffin," said O'Kane, his

tone somewhat macabre, though he had intended it as a joke.

A minute or two of furious laughter and applause ensued. Damián assumed the ratings must be going through the roof. In fact, the director had decided to postpone a commercial break, or possibly even to cancel it; there simply hadn't been a good moment to interrupt this last segment. The audience eventually fell quiet, and Damián recounted how, having hung the clothes up again—in the correct order—he had taken a shower, put on clean boxer shorts and socks belonging to the husband, and donned the tracksuit he had found in the attic.

"And your own clothes?" asked O'Kane. "What did you do with them?"

"Put them inside the built-in wardrobe's drawers. My shoes included, since I'd found a pair of old sneakers along with the tracksuit. The kind of sneakers you wear around the house, and, like the tracksuit, a pretty good fit."

"And then?"

"I whiled away a bit of time. When it got to lunchtime, I fried myself a couple of eggs and made a salad, then cleaned up in the kitchen and again just sat and waited."

"And what kind of thoughts did you have while you, as you say, sat and waited?"

"I had a feeling I'd forgotten something, but I couldn't for the life of me remember what. Actually, I'd been having that sensation ever since I'd awakened that morning."

"You had a lot on your mind," suggested O'Kane.

"Oh, hardly. The opposite, if anything. For example, I only had one message on my cell phone that entire time, from the bank again. My cell can go days, weeks, and not make a sound. I've sometimes called it from my landline to check if it's still working. A lot of people do that when their phone seems to go dead, right? No one ever called me on my landline, either, but—now that I come to think of it, it's strange—it never occurred to me that it might be broken, too."

"We got onto this because you said you felt like you'd forgotten something. Did you work out what it was in the end?"

"Oh, yes, I did."

"And?"

"My acid reflux. It was gone."

7

THE MOTHER and the teenage daughter returned together late in the afternoon.

"I heard a muffled sound," Damián Lobo said to Sergio O'Kane, "which I immediately recognized as that of the garage door opening. It was motorized, and it made a rumbling noise as it folded up against the roof."

"Where were you at that particular moment?"

"In the living room, reading the instruction manual for the extractor fan in the kitchen. I had found the drawer where they kept the instruction manuals for all the appliances in the house."

"And what did you do?" asked O'Kane, trying to keep the interview going in the face of near-continuous laughter from the audience.

"I dashed through into the master bedroom, naturally, climbing into the antique wardrobe and, parting the clothes, through my secret door panel into the built-in wardrobe beyond. I took the extractor fan manual with me, just in case I felt like reading it at any point."

Once again, the audience burst out laughing.

"And then?"

"Then I stayed where I was, quietly listening to the noises around the house, most of which barely registered inside my hiding place, in spite of the fact that I'd left the bedroom door open, as they had done when they went out."

Damián was listening so intently to the sounds in the house that for a few moments he forgot about the TV show entirely. He scrutinized each noise with all the intensity of someone poring over a partially erased text in which letters and entire words were missing. Nonetheless, it was quickly apparent that only the mother and daughter had returned. Perhaps, as was the case in so many families, they had two cars, one big and shiny for the father to drive, and another vehicle, smaller and possibly secondhand, for the wife to get around in.

Damián, on edge as perhaps never before, shuttled manically back and forth between his present reality and the TV show with O'Kane. Being in two places at once wasn't easy. He could hear the women's voices, but not clearly enough to make out what they were saying. The discussions sounded calm, however, the tone like that of normal, practical, day-to-day conversations. He heard doors shutting and opening, footsteps going here and there, the occasional cough, the distant murmur of the television. . . . Then, after an indeterminate amount of time, the mother came into the master bedroom. Damián was aware of her entering and then moving around the room.

"Did she open the wardrobe?" asked O'Kane.

"She did," said Damián. "To change, I assumed. She left the wardrobe door open for a good while, from what I could tell by the alteration in the noises that made it through to me."

"Weren't you worried she'd find the secret door?"

"I wasn't, actually. The beading covered the joins, and the clothes themselves added another layer of concealment, so you couldn't really even see the back panels. I'd been pretty careful."

"You know that when she was taking out an item of clothing, or putting something back in, her hand would have been no more than six inches from where you were?"

"Yes, and we were separated by nothing but a thin sheet of plywood. But in spite of that, it was as though the two of us occupied parallel dimensions—simultaneously very close to each other and very far away."

"Be honest: Weren't you afraid?"

"No, except . . ."

"What?"

"I wondered if this was a kind of invisibility. If God, to put it one way—and I'm not a believer— might exist on the other side of a partition that's as thin as the one that stood between that woman and me."

"And do you think He does?"

"Yes, I think it's quite possible."

"And what else?"

"I could tell she'd gone over to the bed now, leaving, as I say, the middle door of the antique wardrobe open."

A profound silence had descended over the studio audience, so that even the quietest of coughs came through as a roar. One could almost hear the motion of people's eyelashes if they blinked. For a few tenths of a second, O'Kane said nothing, allowing the silence to settle, to thicken, before resuming his questions.

"Did you think you had the right?"

"What harm was I doing?"

"I don't know. Please, go on."

"The woman, as I say, must have changed into a different outfit, and she then shut the wardrobe. Then she went into the bathroom—I heard the toilet flush and then a tap run. She was the kind of person who washes her hands after going to the toilet, exactly as I'd imagined."

Once the laughter at this had died down, O'Kane asked his guest to continue.

"The woman," said Lobo, "came back into the bedroom, and I heard her talking on the phone. I had to open the secret door a crack to be able to hear what she was saying. She was talking to her husband. She asked him if he'd come back to the house at all during the day, the answer to which must have been no.

"'It's really strange,' she said. 'I could've sworn we left the sink full of dishes, and the beds unmade. Or did you actually do all that before we left?'

"The husband," Damián continued, "must have given some explanation or other, something that struck the wife as plausible, because she left it at that. I heard her moving around the bedroom a little while longer, before going out and shutting the door behind her."

"And leaving you sitting there, deep in the darkness."

"That's right. My cell phone had died, which meant I was now completely and utterly isolated from the world, as if I were in a spaceship headed for Mars and had stopped being able to communicate with mission control. I've often spent the time before sleep imagining being in that situation."

"Traveling to Mars?"

"Yes, to Mars."

"To meet new people?" quipped the presenter, drawing a few laughs.

Damián Lobo pondered this.

"I already knew lots of people," he said eventually, visibly irked by Sergio O'Kane's sarcasm. "The point of going to Mars was so I wouldn't have to carry on putting up with them."

"You don't like company very much?"

"I think the best way to describe me is *unusual*."

"Unusual in what sense?"

"In the sense that I'm a good person; I'd never hurt a fly, and this in itself has created distance between me and the rest of the world."

"An inherent benevolence?"

"Yes."

"And the world . . . In your eyes, the world is a bad place?"

"Not just that but dangerous, too."

"And this adventure you had embarked on, was it a way of making the world a better place, making it less dangerous?"

"Possibly. Only time would tell."

"Wouldn't it be more accurate to say you were getting back at it?"

"Getting back at it? I'd never thought of it like that."

"What else happened?"

"The husband came back late, around nine. The first thing I heard was the garage door creaking open. So they did own two cars, as I'd imagined. He came into the house, did something or other for a few minutes, then entered the bedroom, and, like his wife had done, and from what I could make out, changed into some clean clothes. He went out again, and after that any noise started coming from the far end of the house, including the intermittent sound of the TV, and the occasional opening and shutting of doors. I ate the two pieces of fruit I'd had the foresight to bring, along with the fan manual. Then I badly needed to urinate, but there was no way I could use the bathroom, so I went in the washbasin. The family got into their beds at around midnight. They didn't talk much, or in any case didn't discuss anything that might be useful to me. The couple fell asleep with the radio on; after about an hour, one of them must have turned it off. Either that or it turned off automatically."

"Did you have any misgivings about what you were up to?"

"Misgivings? I slept better this second night than the previous one—my little improvised bed turned out to be very comfortable. Good for the back, too, given how hard and flat it was. I woke at around three in the morning, not unusual for me; I never sleep right through the night. The house was silent, and the darkness was absolute. It would have been unthinkable to turn on the light inside the built-in wardrobe—far too likely they'd see. A radio with some headphones would have been great, a good way of combatting my insomnia. I like listening to the radio at night, the kinds of shows where people call in and confess things they'd never tell anyone in broad daylight. The smell of my urine in the washbasin wasn't very nice, so I thought I'd try to organize myself so that in the future I wouldn't need to go to the toilet in the night. I just needed to make sure I didn't drink anything after a certain hour of the day."

"How could you be sure?"

"Erm . . ." Damián cleared his throat. "It's quite a personal thing, but seeing as I've already told you all so much about myself . . . The thing is, I used to wet my bed, into my early teens. . . ."

Damián fell quiet as the laughter rained down from the gallery, even more widespread and thunderous than usual. He guessed from the look on

O'Kane's face that the news from the earpiece was good: more people tuning in. Talk of bodily functions always worked, especially if you apportioned it in the right way. The commotion began to subside, and Damián continued, deploying the same sad-serious expression—always a winner.

"I went to summer camp once; I must have been twelve or thirteen. It was six to a dorm—two triple bunks in each. It would have been a disaster if I'd wet the bed, especially given the fact I had a top bunk. So I started not drinking any liquids after lunchtime, and I even avoided drinking at lunch if we had soup. That meant, if I also stayed vigilant during the night—attentive to any bodily urges—I was able to survive what was a pretty punishing two weeks."

"No bed-wetting at all?"

"No. There was a close call one night, when I had a dream about going to the toilet, but just as I was about to let it out, I realized I was dreaming, and woke up. A couple of drips, that was all. It was then I realized I shouldn't trust my dreams."

Once the laughter in the studio had subsided, O'Kane asked for further details about the first night inside the wardrobe.

"It was just like being a moray eel in some coral hidey-hole. Or like being inside a bubble.

The world was still in motion, planet Earth carried on hurtling through space, while I kind of went my own way. I was like an astronaut in my own little capsule."

"No claustrophobia?"

"None at all. The opposite, in fact: I'd never felt so free. Like my wardrobe was the center of the universe, like the universe was expanding outward from that very point. . . ."

At that moment, around four in the morning, a noise in the bedroom pulled Damián out of the TV show. He put his ear to the panel and, by listening closely, was able to tell that the wife or husband had gotten up to use the toilet. He heard the toilet flush, but no tap running, from which he surmised it must be the husband—unlike the wife, not the kind to wash his hands after using the toilet.

The room was soon quiet again, and Damián felt Sergio O'Kane urging him back to the television studio, but he resisted. The endless discussion, exposing his life for the cameras, was starting to wear on him. And when he found the show wearing, the interview was bound to become less interesting. When the intensity wavered like this, the show became unconvincing, the same way a novel or a film can be unconvincing. And then it simply dropped away, disappeared altogether, for all that Damián could hear O'Kane calling to him. But the longer he spent away from the show, the greater his enthusiasm would be when he went back to it; it was as though the fantasy was bolstered, reinforced somehow, in the absence of his undivided attention.

He did not return to the interview that night. He fell asleep at around five in the morning, and woke again at quarter to seven, when the radio came on and the garbled sound of the news filtered through to his hiding place. The house came to life in a series of repeat morning rituals. Once the family had gone, Damián climbed out of the wardrobes, emptied the container into which he'd urinated, ate some breakfast, washed the dishes, made the beds, had a shower, put on some clean underwear—placing the previous day's boxer shorts and socks in a laundry basket he found in the daughter's bathroom—and proceeded to search the cupboards for any information that might help him to survive the strange world in which he found himself.

PART
TWO

8

BEING A MAN of habit, Damián had little trouble adapting to the routine of the home where he had landed, the upkeep of which he gradually took upon himself. So, as well as making the beds and washing the dishes, he started cooking supper, too, with whatever ingredients he happened to find in the fridge. Washing and ironing days were soon added to his schedule. On Mondays, he vacuumed, and Wednesdays and Fridays were for dusting. After four or five weeks, he had taken on virtually all the tasks necessary for the maintenance of such a home.

Although he took on new chores only when it seemed the family had stopped noticing everything he was already doing—not wishing to ring any alarm bells—the older woman, Lucía, did seem to pick up on the changes. In the world of the husband and daughter, it was simply the norm that someone else should be dealing with domestic duties. Either they didn't ask themselves who that someone was or they assumed it was the mother. Or at least this was Damián's assumption, based on what he could make out from inside the wardrobe.

One day, not long after he had installed himself in the house, he overheard a phone conversation between Lucía, sitting on the bed, by the sound of it, and her mother. Once the preliminary hellos were over, it sounded as though Lucía wanted to fill her mother in on something but felt hesitant. Eventually, and falteringly, she broached the subject.

"If I tell you something, Mamá, will you promise not to laugh? . . . Do you remember I told you about finding Grandma and Grandpa's wardrobe in an antiques market? . . . Yes, it goes really nicely in the house; we put it in our bedroom. Also, it's so spacious; you can fit far more into it than we could in the built-in one, which we've effectively had to write off. . . . There just wasn't any other wall to put it against. But anyway, what I was saying was, you won't believe it, but the day the wardrobe came through the front door, some kind of *presence*—I don't know how to describe it—it was like some kind of good spirit entered the house. . . . How can I tell? I can tell because the house is less of a bomb site. It's like it's started tidying itself. . . . See, I knew you'd laugh. . . . No, no, I knew you'd be like that about it. . . . Laugh all you like, but it's been a lifesaver for me. This house is far harder to run than the apartment was, and we had to let the cleaning lady go—you know how I had a pay cut, and it isn't going well at the store. In fact, it's going badly at the store. . . . Fede? Fede couldn't fry an egg. He doesn't have a clue about the dishwasher or the washing machine. And María, the age she's at . . . I haven't told you, Ma, but María's having a hard time. I didn't say anything because I didn't want you to worry, but . . . Eating problems. It isn't that serious—lots of girls have issues around this age—but what with that and one or two other things . . . She just isn't doing that great. None of us is, to tell the truth. . . . No, I'll tell you all about it. . . . The weather? Well, it's been lovely and warm— we've turned the heating off—but it's been raining pretty much every day, and I don't just mean the odd shower. They're saying it's the wettest April since sometime or other in the last century."

The woman's phone conversations in the bedroom, coupled with Damián's detective work around the house, allowed him to start forming a picture of the family members. Each left his or her particular traces, and had his or her own problems, which, in turn, related to those of the others in a strange interweaving of encounters and misunderstandings that constituted the fabric of this family. Never had he put a family under the microscope like this before, not even his own, and he found the results surprising and difficult to fathom.

He soon ascertained that Fede, the father, owned and managed an electronic toy store in a mall. Also, that the mother worked for a bakery chain known for its artisanal breads and pastries. He learned that they'd been married for fifteen years, and that María, the teenage daughter, on whose computer he had found a secret diary, which he skimmed—with the unpleasant sense of this being a violation—was the only girl in her class yet to start her period. This was a worry and a relief to her in equal measure: she was disgusted by the idea of bleeding, but at the same time she was anxious about being the odd one out among her peers. In any case, she had tricked her parents into believing that she had in fact started, dipping tampons in some kind of red substance at the same time each month and leaving them in the bathroom trash.

Damián shared little of this with Sergio O'Kane, from whom he had started to distance himself. He wasn't spending as much time in the TV studio now, and had become less forthcoming in his answers. The progressive estrangement came down to the fact that the presenter, perhaps envious of Damián's rising star in the media, had started trying to occupy center stage. His questions were invariably dripping with irony, and at times he even set out to trip Damián up, also insinuating his guest might have mental problems. Though aware that O'Kane existed only in his mind, Damián had begun to resent him, which struck him as both strange and altogether reasonable.

The family routine changed on weekends. The father worked at the toy store all day on Saturdays, while mother and daughter tended either to put their feet up at home or go for groceries at a supermarket that must have been nearby. Damián noticed they had a tendency to buy more than they needed. Impulse shoppers—that was how he decided to define them—lacking the capacity to plan. They bought chicken wings by the dozen, only for them to spoil in the fridge, and the same went for the various vegetables and cheeses, the layers of mold on which it was necessary to penetrate to access the edible parts. The day he cleaned the fridge, he found fermented yogurts and decomposing sauces that must have been lurking untouched for months. By his calculations, with the money they would have saved by shopping in a more efficient manner, they could have afforded to bring back their cleaning lady.

After the Saturday siesta, the daughter often went out with friends, and the mother would either stay at home or go to the toy store to lend a hand. The couple sometimes came home late, either alone or with the daughter, whom they had presumably collected from the cinema or a friend's house. If they weren't the ones collecting her themselves, she was under strict instructions always to be home no later than ten thirty, and she tended to comply. On occasion, she stayed over at a friend's, or a friend would come to stay the night at her house.

As for Sundays, it was not unusual for friends or relatives to come over for lunch, nor for these meals to last well into the early evening. They sometimes went out for Sunday lunch; Damián could not always tell where to, given how little he could hear from inside the wardrobe, and anyway, conversation was minimal between the husband and wife once they were in the bedroom. In any case, they tended not to stay out late on Sundays because the daughter was expected to spend the latter part of the day studying.

If they had no guests, the family ate in the living room, watching the news on television. The mother and father divided their afternoons and evenings between television and household chores, including gardening, which Damián avoided, for fear of being seen by one of the neighbors or caught on a satellite camera. They were not a family of readers, because there were no books in the house, apart from the pile in the attic concerning questions of the paranormal, which, presumably, harkened back to a time when Fede or Lucía—more likely Lucía—had taken an interest in the subject.

One day, O'Kane asked Damián why he had resisted establishing the location of the house, to which he replied that, if he had found out, it would have broken the spell.

"Spell?" O'Kane laughed. "What did this situation—in which you were clearly committing a criminal act, by the way—have to do with spells?"

The allusion to criminality struck Damián as inappropriate, so he stood up and walked out of the studio, leaving O'Kane mid-conversation. It was not the first time he had done so, to the despair of his interviewer, who had been watching the show's ratings plummet as its true star lost interest.

The family operated in accordance with well-established patterns, and though mother, father, and daughter rarely argued, displays of affection were similarly rare. In the absence of love, they operated on the basis of an unspoken pact of cohabitation, as though, rather than a home, the trio had found themselves in the lounge of a train station, all three awaiting trains to take them away, sooner or later, to separate destinations.

The man and the woman had sex rarely, and it was always a case of going through the motions. Their exclamations and sighs, far from exciting Damián, produced a cool sensation in him somewhere between indifference and surprise. And so, while the pair progressed toward orgasm (like trains running on parallel tracks, ultimately headed for different termini), he, in the depths of the wardrobe, wondered if his life would have been like theirs had he been able to adapt to the customs of normal people.

He imagined himself as a father, running a toy store, but felt skeptical: Could he? Could he really? Whereas being a part of this group in the guise of a ghost was something he found he enjoyed. None of the other roles would have fit him. Husband, wife, daughter—he wasn't cut out for any of these. The only function he felt he could fulfill was that of a kindly poltergeist willingly keeping house, which was a branch of maintenance.

He sometimes wondered how long the situation might last. He fantasized about it lasting forever. And about things progressing, too, in the sense of a day arriving when he would be able to step out of the wardrobe and move among them, while remaining invisible. They would all be in the kitchen, living room, hall, all four of them at the same time, but the other three would not see him.

The mother's gratitude for his attentions was not lost on Damián: she was obviously happier now than when he'd moved in. She had brought down a number of the paranormal books from the attic, which she read with pen in hand, underlining copiously as she went, before hiding the volumes at the back of the antique wardrobe—inches from Damián's location—where neither the husband nor the daughter would find them. Damián read them, and was particularly interested in which sections she'd chosen to underline—in one way or another, they were about him. Him as an individual from another dimension, who nonetheless has the capacity to affect this one.

And as he came to identify more and more with beings that return from the afterlife to help their loved ones, he found less need to spend time in O'Kane's company. A day came when Damián decided never to go back to the show, and soon after this he learned that it had been discontinued due to woeful viewing figures. Picturing the former star presenter begging his bosses for scraps, going around pleading for something to do on the channel where he'd once been the main attraction, Damián felt that a specific kind of retribution had been exacted. Deeply involved as he was in his new life, he did not examine why he hated a person who existed only inside his mind.

9

MAY CAME, and the rains continued. Damián found it quite dazzling; never before had rain affected him in this way. Sometimes, after finishing his tasks around the house, he would stand at a window and lose himself while looking out at the torrents, until a downpour began inside him, as well. The storms were accompanied by a strange light, also something he had never seen, and which felt somehow like a reflection of his personal state. The plants in the garden burst forth at an amazing speed.

The books on ghosts and apparitions, which he read enthusiastically, replaced the appliance manuals and the instruction booklets Fede brought back from the shop when he needed to examine the functioning of certain especially complicated toys. And though he'd never been interested in the supernatural, the stories in these volumes awoke a hitherto-unknown delight. He did not so much read the words as imbibe them, savoring them, turning them over in his mouth, before letting them drop down inside him, where they continued to exert a strange suggestive power.

One day, after learning from one of these books about the existence of a ghost that specialized in dispatching children who did not wash their hands before mealtimes, he shut his eyes and saw an image of a young boy going into the bathroom of his house and using the toilet, and then merely letting the tap run for a few moments, so as to trick his parents. Saw him come out of the bathroom, to a congratulatory smile from his mother and father, and walk down the hallway with a teddy bear in his arms—unaware of the presence of the ghost, whose job it was to tear both their heads off, his and the teddy bear's. The words in those books, with the incessant rain drumming in the background, conjured images in Damián's mind of a startling coherence, which even the former visions of the TV studio where Sergio O'Kane reigned would have been hard-pressed to match.

The phantasmagorical possessed an unwonted corporeality now. The dead circulated in the world of the living as naturally as water running from the taps, or lightbulbs coming on at the flick of a switch. Diving into one of these books was enough to cause the normal bounds of reality to shift, paving the way for the entrance of vague but undeniably real presences. He was himself one such presence; he, who until recently had lived under the same enslavements as ordinary mortals, now began to expand beyond the limits of his body, functioning as a kind of demon in the world of the living, but especially in the world of Lucía, the woman of the house, over whom he cast his protective shadow.

It wasn't long before Damián took on some of the qualities of apparitions, those who have returned to this world or who never managed to depart, either because they failed to find the way out or were prevented by some unresolved matter. Perhaps he had been drawn to this house, and this wardrobe, by invisible forces swirling around the piece of furniture itself. Perhaps he was the agent of these forces, or perhaps, as he had read in one of the discussions of inexplicable happenings, it's the living who do the bidding of the deceased. Not all living beings—the selection is far from random. A certain level of intelligence is a basic prerequisite, as is a finer sensibility of the kind from which he had always benefited, or perhaps suffered.

He sometimes came away from these intense reading sessions a touch feverish. He felt compelled to respond to the marks the woman had made in the books by underlining certain phrases himself; and so now a curious dialogue arose between the two of them. At first, he did no more than highlight those phrases and ideas that jumped out at him, or which, in one way or another, seemed particularly to speak to their shared situation. This soon gave way to his under-lining discrete letters and individual words that combined to make new phrases altogether.

"Who are you?" she wrote on one of the pages, following his lead by circling the letters that made up the question and numbering them to indicate their order.

"Are you sure you don't know?" he replied, fol-lowing the same procedure.

"I think I might," she wrote. "Have you come to save me?"

"From what?"

He always kept his answers short, convinced that pithiness was more likely to give an impres-sion of intelligence than long-windedness.

"Are all ghosts intelligent?" the woman wrote one day.

"All intelligent people have a ghostly aspect," he wrote in reply, turning the question back on itself, a lesson he had learned from his father, who had always been a great lover of wordplay.

This was also a way of making himself seem

enigmatic, crucial if he was to maintain his position. The inherent difficulty in communicating like this forced them to be brief in any case, which for now was to Damián's advantage.

"What did you do today?" asked Lucía.

"The important thing is what I have undone," he replied.

Before long, he began combining his readings about the world of the uncanny with internet searches on the daughter's computer. The only marks he left were his fingerprints, which were invisible to the naked eye anyway. One day, while sitting at the computer, he coughed, leaving tiny specks of saliva on the screen, and, secure in the sensation that they had mixed with María's own expectorations, he did not wipe them off. He sometimes thought that as he moved around the house he would perhaps be leaving a faint trail of his body odor behind, as well as microscopic flakes of skin from his body or his scalp.

He didn't miss tobacco at all, though he'd been an addict for years. He came to understand that with each inhalation, back when he smoked, he was searching for the one that would cause him damage, but it always seemed to lie in the next cigarette down the line, and so he would smoke one after another, without the damage ever transpiring, or at least not to the degree he'd been imagining. It would, he thought, have been the same for alcoholics and whatever they consumed: every drink was a question of trying to land the one that, far from making the person's head spin, would illuminate that individual in some final, conclusive way. But that illumination lay forever in the next bottle, the next glass. Now, each time he thought about taking a drag, but did not in fact take one—occasions he could enumerate because he had gone so far as to count them—a kind of inverse illumination took place inside him, one he likewise sought to decipher.

His hair had grown long, as had his beard; he had not dared to use Fede's electric razor, given how different their hair was. Fede would be bound to notice someone else's shorn stubble inside the mechanism. He looked not unlike a ghostly Robinson Crusoe.

He scoured the internet for ghost stories, he watched videos, and he looked at photographs. How, he wondered, could he have spent so long completely ignorant of this other world, one that was clearly real? He was put in mind of his life to date, and how—he now saw—so much had happened that was extravagant, singular, incredible, to the extent that no explanation would do other than that a larger scheme was in operation, one he'd had no choice but to go along with.

There were endless forums about ghosts and apparitions. Most were fairly dull, owing to the fact that the people posting on them were either clearly unhinged or simply had too much time on their hands. But he came across the occasional chat room in which people recounted their experiences with both sincerity and astonishment.

He was deeply struck by the case of one young woman who wrote that, walking along her hallway one day, she had "felt a current of air that seemed like it scooped everything out from inside me and replaced it with everything that existed in the world." Damián had experienced something similar one night inside the wardrobe, when he'd felt claustrophobia encroaching but overcame it with the aid of a perception that fit the description on the forum: it had struck him that, though it seemed otherwise, he was not inside the wardrobe, wasn't even inside the world, but, rather, the wardrobe and the world existed inside him.

On the same forum, a man had posted something that described his bus ride to work one day, and how his cell phone had started ringing in his pocket. He took the device out, only to find that in fact it was not ringing—and yet the ringing sound went on. So he got his wallet out, to discover that this was actually the source of the noise. Opening it up, he found that the sound was coming from a photograph of his dead daughter; there was a landline phone in the background. This was where the noise was coming from, but of course there was no way for him to reach into the image and pick it up. Who was the call for? he asked himself. For the dead girl? For him? And who might have been calling? From that day on, the man wrote, the telephone started to ring regularly, sometimes in the middle of the night, plunging the dead girl's father into feelings of impotence, not to mention desperation.

What everyone on these forums had in common was that they were human beings. For some reason, ghosts never posted anything about their experiences in the world of the living. It therefore took him a long time, in his capacity as ghost, to decide to intervene. Eventually, a morning came when he sat down and, clicking through to the forum he felt most confident about, and feeling extremely apprehensive, he began to write:

"I am one of the ghosts you have all been writing about here. I live in a house with a family whose members, obviously, cannot see me. But they benefit from my being here all the same. Unlike most of the spirits I see people writing about on this forum, I make myself useful. I don't go around rapping on things or turning the lights off and on, and I don't take things and put them where they aren't supposed to be. It has fallen to me to make this family's life better, to help them. Whenever they go out, I take care of all the domestic tasks, and generally see to the upkeep of the place. It helps that I am an expert when it comes to fixing things. I would be interested to know if any other ghosts out there find themselves in a situation similar to my own. I would love to compare notes."

In an involuntary flourish of humor, of the kind that had served him so well in the interviews with Sergio O'Kane, he signed off as "Ghost Butler," an alias that proved an instant hit on the forum. Replies came flooding in, most of them mocking in tone. But as he responded to each with his customary seriousness, it wasn't long before people began taking him seriously, too, ushering in a period of attention and fame that, unlike his time in the limelight alongside O'Kane, was real, given that it took place not solely inside his head.

He was asked about his experience, what it was like to be him, and he answered honestly but prudently. Yes, he said, he was the kind of ghost that lodged inside a piece of furniture, in the same way other spirits were associated with and

centered their activities around a particular building or room. He avoided mentioning what piece
of furniture, in case anyone should come looking
for him. For the same reasons, he went into little
detail about the family in which he had "embed-
ded" himself.

"Please forgive me," he wrote at one point. "I
cannot divulge the location of the family whose
home it is, or anything that might enable anyone
to find me. Any such attentions would be most
unwelcome."

Ghost Butler was immediately the talk of
numerous associated forums. A journalist special-
izing in consumer news picked up the story, and
it was soon repeated on several radio breakfast
shows. Damián listened with growing astonishment while he did the morning cleaning. Though
many of the listeners called in to mock the idea,
one show dedicated to discussions of the paranormal gave it respectful and considered attention.

During the nights, stretching out as best he
could inside the built-in wardrobe, and vigilant as
ever for sounds in the house, he began to see that
Sergio O'Kane—who still occasionally showed up,
begging to be brought back to life—had been a mere
staging post on his ascent to the popularity he was
now enjoying, which he needed to handle using

real-world resources. The interesting part was that these same resources became more numerous in line with his progress into true ghosthood. It was true that, with the passing of the days, he was progressively becoming less and less flesh and bone, or so it seemed to him.

He still used his body to move around, of course, and he continued to keep this body hidden, so that none of the family would see him, but at the same time his physical needs were diminishing. He was eating less, on certain days next to nothing, though he had developed a great love of water, a substance he identified with due to its transparency, its capacity for evaporation, and the ease with which it could change shape.

In his new state, far removed from earthly concerns, he sometimes recalled his past existence, and it struck him as quite amazing that he could have spent so long trapped in the fictitious freedom of the outside world. Paradoxically, it was only now, with so much of his life spent curled up inside the wardrobe, that he felt free. This new kind of liberty was marked by great mental fluidity, his thoughts flowing where they would, as though just one more bodily secretion. And the universe had become glasslike, everything transparent to him, for all that it was rooted in a world he found opaque, a place where he had often felt compelled to doubt his own intelligence.

He sometimes cast his mind back to his father and to his Chinese sister, Desirée. He could picture them in their well-appointed apartment in Arturo Soria, watching another Iñaki Gabilondo interview on Canal+, seeking out old movies on that same subscription channel, or reading nineteenth-century Russians. He thought of his dead mother, who had possibly died of jealousy. How many such domestic crimes happened every day—or week, or month—in a city like Madrid?

Then Damián had a sudden vision that seemed to him all too real: He was presented with an image of an unexceptional apartment block, but one allowing a view into each of the homes inside it. It was like a cross section of an ants' nest, the kind that gave you a window into the creatures' behavior. The behavior of human beings in the kitchen, in the bathroom, in the living room. A woman changing her tampon, a man lifting weights, a teenage boy masturbating in the mirror. . . .

Then his father's behavior toward Damián's adopted sister, Desirée, came to mind. For a moment, Damián wondered if he had imagined the whole thing.

Indeed, he had only the vaguest memories,

if any at all, of Desirée menstruating. Either she must have been very discreet about the whole thing or he, with his head in the clouds as usual, must not have noticed. If he could have talked to his Chinese sister now, he would have asked how old she was when she got her period. He could have used that to help María, Fede and Lucía's daughter, in her current tribulations. What would it be like to wait for your period to come? As he wondered about this, a picture came to him of the teenage girl: she was standing, legs braced, eyes possibly closed, and listening to the blood circulating in her veins and arteries, its rhythmic, recurrent motion, like a train passing through a tunnel.

But what if something had happened in his absence? What if his father had died, for instance? He was certainly old enough. How would they have gone about resolving the inheritance? Do some elderly people approach death with the same anxiety as girls awaiting their period?

By some miracle, he had managed to keep his Chinese sister out of his sexual fantasies of late. These now revolved around Lucía, though it was true that, just at the moment of ejaculation, in the very final second, her face often morphed into Desirée's.

Would his father and sister have been wondering

where he had gone, what he was doing, why he didn't answer their calls? Would they even have thought about him? He liked the idea they might have accepted their fates in the same way he had surrendered himself to the workings of chaos. For his current existence was precisely this: a product of the chaos that, in his former life, he had always sought to obviate—so misguidedly. He had read this in one of the books on the paranormal, in a chapter entitled "Finding the Good in Chaos: The Benefits of Giving Up Control." It was now normal for him to be out of control, out of the world, existing, in fact, in a kind of next world, one where he had finally found the correct way to engage with this one.

It was in the wardrobe one night, as a tremendous storm raged outside, that he realized how wrong he'd been to sign his posts on the forum as Ghost Butler. Was it not, in fact, humiliating to associate oneself with the social order in that way? And when others referred to him as such—on the forum, on the radio, and doubtless on the worst kind of TV shows imaginable—was it a way of making themselves feel superior? Was he condemned to spend his days like this, eking out this lowly, parasitic existence, of which now, deep in his hiding place, he suddenly felt very ashamed?

10

ON THE FORUM Damián visited most often, dozens of posts started appearing daily from people claiming to be the beneficiaries of Ghost Butler's visitations.

"He lives in my parents' bedside table," said some.

"I've felt him in the garbage room of my building," declared others.

Damián always replied to these messages, asking people to post something that only he and that individual could know. Of course, nobody ever could, until one day someone—user name "Grateful"—posted a message saying, "Dear Ghost Butler, I think it's me you've been looking after."

And when Damián made his usual request for proof, Grateful described, in some detail, the dinner the ghost had cooked for her and her family the previous night.

So, in their excitement, heads throbbing, Ghost Butler and Grateful withdrew from the public board to continue conversing in the intimacy of direct messages.

Damián wanted to know whether Lucía's husband and daughter were aware of his presence; the possibility worried him.

"Only slightly," she wrote, "if at all. When it began, I mentioned it—that a benevolent presence had come into the house at the same time as my grandparents' wardrobe—and they both thought it was a big joke. But later on, as it became clear to me you really did exist, and not wanting to share you now, I made light of my previous assertions. They both know I have an interest in the world of the paranormal, but they've never taken it seriously."

"So who do they think has been doing all the chores?" he replied.

"Me. Food on the table, clean clothes, beds made—that's as far as the questions go for them. I've also spent quite a lot of time getting rid of evidence, anything that screams out that you've been here. It would actually be better if you didn't do so much; otherwise, they're bound to suspect. I sometimes end up having to do twice as much, just to make it seem like everything you've done is my work."

"Wouldn't it be better if they simply accepted my presence?" he asked.

"But I already said I don't want to share you with anyone. And I mean it. I want you for myself."

Damián felt so moved by this that it was as if she had whispered it in his ear, not typed it on a computer. Since he knew her voice, it was easy to imagine the words being softly spoken. It was eleven in the morning. By his calculations, Fede would be at the toy store, María at school, and Lucía at the bakery. The only person in the house was the one who did not belong there: him. And he was now struck by the sheer oddness of the situation; here he was, an intruder in the bedroom of a girl whose bed he had just made and whose panties he had not long before dropped in the laundry basket. Here he was, incredibly, passing himself off as a ghost while the world outside continued—it was as if the real world were a bus, continuing on its way, and he had simply alighted. What if he were to go back to that communal existence, business as usual, before things got out of hand?

It would be perfectly possible for him to cut short the conversation with Lucía then and there, turn off the computer, leave the bedroom, walk down the hall, open the front door, and step back out into the world, like a person reborn. His life out there would still be intact (as long as his father had not died, that is). There would still be funds in his bank account from his settlement package, his unemployment checks would also have been going in, and all his utility bills, plus the installments for his TV and the car, would have continued to be serviced.

He pictured his car, which he had left parked on the corner nearest to his apartment building and which would by now be gathering dust. He had never driven it much anyway, and almost not at all once he'd lost his job; it was something he owned for the sake of it, and he'd had to make an effort to park it in different places so people wouldn't mistake it for an abandoned vehicle; he'd sometimes taken it out onto the freeway, any freeway, just to charge the battery.

This vision of the car was followed by another of his apartment standing empty, the mortgage of which he had finished paying off the previous year. It had three rooms (kitchen/living room, bedroom, bathroom) and was a stone's throw from the Usera subway stop, in the neighborhood where most of Madrid's Chinese population resided. He had bought it for a song; it was very run-down and had needed renovating completely, a job he had done himself. Weekend after weekend he had spent ripping up floorboards and putting in new partition walls, installing new plumbing, doing all of the painting and wallpapering himself, varnishing the doors, and modernizing the electrical system, along with a remodeling of both the bathroom and kitchen. And even after all of that, he had carried on adding touches that increased the property's value. He had put it up for sale at one point out of curiosity, and, though never intending to sell, he was offered close to three times what he had bought it for.

He saw his old life, and knew it was not too late to go back there, but it seemed very alien to him. There would be no difficulty in laying claim to these things, as he had all the necessary paperwork, and yet, in spite of the brush of panic he had just experienced, it was not something he could see himself doing.

"Are you still there?" wrote the woman.

"I am," he replied.

"I'm at work at the moment," she continued. "I was in the car this morning after dropping my daughter off at school, and I heard about Ghost Butler on the radio. I knew straightaway it was you. It had to be. Why did you choose to go public like this?"

"I don't know," wrote Damián. "I get bored."

"And why are you the only spirit ever to have manifested on the internet?"

"I'm a trailblazer," he typed, sensing this might be a silly thing to say, more apt to the O'Kane show than to a conversation with Lucía; she surely would not take it seriously.

"One other thing: Was it a coincidence that you showed up at the same time as my grandparents' wardrobe?"

". . ."

"Well, was it?"

"I would rather not reveal myself," he replied.

"What computer are you using?"

"I don't need an actual computer. . . . I'm sorry, but I have to go now."

"Can we write to each other here again?"

"Okay. I'll come onto the forum at the same time tomorrow. Write me then."

"One more thing: Please stop making my daughter's bed. I always have to mess it up again. I've been trying to get her to make her own bed and generally tidy up after herself for years. Your help . . . doesn't help. Plus, I hardly have any time between getting back myself and her coming home; it's always a mad dash."

"Will do."

Damián logged off and took a breath. Another

two minutes and he knew he would have gone to pieces. He was sweating and out of breath, as if he'd been engaged in some punishing physical exercise. Once he had recovered, he got up from the chair, tottering slightly and feeling weak, as though recovering from an illness, then went through into the master bedroom, undressing and getting into the bed on the wife's side. The sheets were cold, but he could still smell the lotion Lucía used at night, little jars of which he had found in the bathroom cupboard. He closed his eyes and tried to re-create the brief conversation they had just been having.

He got out of the bed. His naked, bony figure went through to the guest room, where Lucía kept her underwear in the wardrobe. Until now, he had respected this space, and hardly touched her panties or bras at all—only when absolutely necessary for doing the washing and ironing. He had acted respectfully toward these garments, maintaining the same sort of distance as he did with the world at large. But this distance had broken now, just as something inside him had broken.

"What happened next?" asked Sergio O'Kane, who always pounced anytime Damián was feeling confused or unsure.

"I took a slightly worn lingerie set and went back to the bed," he said.

"What color was it?"

"Well, tobacco-colored, or maybe flesh-colored, I guess."

"To masturbate over?" asked O'Kane.

The laughter among members of the studio audience snatched Damián out of his reverie; it made him feel dirty. How, he asked himself as he got under the sheets again, how could he have been a part of this trashy display of TV boorishness, and for so long? And though it had indeed been his idea to masturbate, he now decided against it, and, still clutching Lucía's undergarments to him, he spat out aggressively, "Look, I just want you to leave me alone, get it? My interviews with you were completely imaginary. You aren't real."

"So I guess you think you're more real now than when you used to come on my show."

"I do, actually."

"A 'real ghost'?"

"That's exactly what I am. A real ghost."

"But there's no such thing."

"It's you there's no such thing as."

"How come you're talking to me, then?"

"Habit. Now go away."

"How about you agree to just come on the show once a week?" O'Kane said, begging now.

"No," said Damián. "Not with this audience, not

with this trashy viewership. I'm a different person now, but you're exactly the same."

The conversation with O'Kane, with all the old emotions it conjured, felt exhausting to Damián, wearing in the extreme. It carried on gnawing away at him, dragging him down until he was close to sleep, lying in a bed that did not belong to him, stretched out in the bodily impression of a woman who was not Chinese, and surrounded by all the sounds and all the silence of the house in which his new identity had been forged.

11

"**D**O YOU EAT FOOD?" the woman asked Damián the next day in a private message on the forum.

Was this a trick question? He did eat—less and less, but he still ate, and if Lucía were even the slightest bit observant, she must have noticed. But did ghosts eat? Hesitating, he cast his mind back to the books of hers he had read, before eventually typing his reply.

"Do you know what it is a ghost misses most?"

"The body," wrote the woman.

"That's right. The ether is crowded with spirits desperately looking for bodies to occupy. Because of this, because we yearn so terribly to have our bodies back, we play at eating, and at taking showers, and even at cutting our fingernails and toenails. There's no way for us to leave clippings from our fingernails or toenails, but we can make the food we're pretending to eat disappear."

"I thought so!" wrote Lucía, and Damián could

hear her voice with such clarity, exclaiming these words. He had little difficulty picturing her speaking the words, given how minutely he had studied the photographs of her in the house.

And it was true, at least according to the books he had read and all the articles on the internet: the absence of a body drove ghosts to distraction, like heroin addicts being deprived of a fix. The dependency on the body was far harder to kick than any drug. But in Damián Lobo's case, he was in the process of detaching himself from his body, and all too happily.

Again he heard the woman's voice in his head—*I thought so!*—only this time the tone was far more seductive, like a whisper in his ear, like a sweet nothing. . . . Several seconds elapsed, and then Lucía sent another message:

"When I first started noticing things, signs of you being here, I thought I'd gone crazy. I thought a part of me was making the beds, washing the dishes, and putting the washing machine on so that another part of me would have a chance to believe in ghosts. You also can't imagine how disconcerted I was when I came across the wardrobe in the antiques market."

"Why? What happened in this wardrobe?"

When her reply appeared on the screen, Damián

Lobo had barely begun reading before he felt a pang for Sergio O'Kane. He hadn't yet found anything to replace that listening presence, and there were moments when he felt badly in need of someone to whom he could recount his experience. Now was one such moment. And so, like a person trying to make a decision at the edge of a precipice, just as he was about to let go of the branch he was clinging to, he imagined Iñaki Gabilondo sitting across from him in the interviewer's chair, in a more dignified studio, and with a smaller, more select audience than on the O'Kane show.

"What did the woman say about the wardrobe?" asked the award-winning journalist.

"She told me that it had belonged to her grandparents, who were farmers in a village near Santander, and that she and her brother, Jorge, had played in it when they were small. They had been sent to live with their grandparents while their mother got over a mystery illness that ended up keeping her bedridden for five years. Lucía and Jorge were twins, but not identical, because they had come from separate eggs. Her brother, she pointed out, had been born with the index finger of his right hand missing—the grandfather used to joke that he'd eaten it while they were still inside their mother's belly. So when they climbed into the wardrobe, they would take off their clothes and carry on where they'd left off in the womb. They played a game in which he ate her finger, and another in which they played at being each other."

"And what else?" Gabilondo prompted his interviewee, who was looking pensive and had fallen quiet.

"Oh," said Damián, coming to his senses, "the brother died of tetanus at age seven, after getting a cut in the stables and the grandparents failing to clean it properly."

"Go on," Gabilondo pressed him.

"Well, she carried on playing in the wardrobe—inside it, around it, anywhere in its vicinity. She spent hours on end opening and shutting the door, hoping to find her brother hiding between her grandmother's dresses and her grandfather's jackets."

"Old wardrobes, and childhood," the journalist interjected, at which point Damián noticed that the man across from him had turned into Sergio O'Kane.

It had taken mere moments for O'Kane to return, in the same way that Damián's sexual fantasies—for all that he had been trying to recast them—always ended up returning to the same limited, worn-out repertoire of Chinese faces and bodies. But before he knew it, and before he could try to call Gabilondo back to the TV studio, Lucía had typed another message about the wardrobe. Damián grudgingly accepted that it was O'Kane he would have to talk to.

"Old wardrobes, and childhood," repeated the yellow-eyed journalist as Damián tried to get his words out.

"Yes," he said. "But she had another tragic story associated with the wardrobe."

"We're on the edge of our seats," said O'Kane, gesturing to the audience members, who were indeed holding their breath.

"Lucía's grandparents worried about her playing with the wardrobe so much. They worried she would shut her fingers in one of the doors. 'Mind your fingers!' she would always hear them say when she was playing in their bedroom. They called out from the kitchen, from the dining room, from the hallway, and sometimes they would be in the bedroom with her and say it. 'Mind your fingers!' This obsession with fingers penetrated so deeply into the little girl's brain that one day, while the grandparents dozed in front of the TV, she went into their bedroom, walked up to the wardrobe, positioned herself in front of its middle portion, and, looking her reflection in the eye, opened the middle door with her left hand, placed the forefinger of her right hand in the gap by the hinges, and slammed the door on it with surprising force. She says she heard the crack of the bone snapping but that it didn't hurt; it was more like an anesthetized limb being operated on: she was aware of it, but not in a painful way. Then, after an inexplicable lull, it hit her. She screamed, and immediately passed out. When she came to, her hand was in bandages, and after a short while she was told—to avoid her being frightened when they changed the dressing—that she wouldn't be getting her forefinger back. 'This one,' said the grandmother, holding out her own."

O'Kane held his breath; the people in the audience held their breath. Damián imagined the ratings must be sky-high. But Lucía carried on typing, leaving no time for O'Kane's beloved dramatic pauses. Damián went on retelling the story as he saw the words appear on the screen.

"The grandmother decided to get rid of the wardrobe, says Lucía. It was like a family deciding to get rid of a dog after it's bitten someone. The wardrobe was taken to an outbuilding that housed chickens and rabbits. And to stop it from biting anyone again, they took the doors off, wrapped them in brown paper, and left them in some remote corner of the farm. They encased the main part of the wardrobe in cardboard, but the animals soon took up residence inside it. It became one more chicken coop, and a place they particularly liked to huddle inside on cold days."

"And so?" O'Kane said, urging Damián to continue.

"Lucía says she would now go and stand in front of the wardrobe, and instead of seeing her reflection—the mirror had been taken off—all she saw was an enormous chasm. It was like the wardrobe had swallowed her reflection, she says. Things also started disappearing inside the wardrobe, going in but not coming back out again: some hens' eggs, a number of rabbits, even one chicken Lucía was particularly fond of and that used to follow her around."

"So things the family used to cook and eat?" asked O'Kane.

"I guess so. Lucía says that her grandfather, to cover up the disappearances, started putting things in the wardrobe and taking them out when she wasn't around."

"Such as?" O'Kane asked.

"An old doll she had, which she called Jorge. She says . . . she says she used to talk to it as though it were her dead brother, and that her grandparents were worried about this. When the wardrobe swallowed the doll, she accepted it, but her grandfather also said that everything that disappeared into the depths of the wardrobe would one day come back—from wherever it had gone. Lucía grew up believing this fantastical idea to be wholly the truth—hence her agitation when she came across the wardrobe in the market."

Having given a hurried account of the wardrobe's history, Lucía wrote that she had to get back to work. Before logging off, she told Ghost Butler that she would be going away the next day, to the village in Santander, in fact, to visit her sick mother, and that she would be gone for a few days. She would be taking María with her, since she didn't trust Fede to look after her properly, what with the amount of time he spent at the store. María was having some eating problems, she added, and she wanted to keep a close eye on her. She asked Ghost Butler to please desist from all housework while she was gone, for fear her husband might suspect.

"Will there be any way for us to communicate?" wrote Damián.

"No," she replied. "There's no internet at my mother's house, and barely any signal in the village."

"The relationship between the two of you was becoming almost adulterous," said O'Kane, to the audience's delight.

PART
THREE

12

ALTHOUGH THE HOUSE stirred at the usual hour the next morning, Damián Lobo, lodged inside his cave, could tell things were different: the kind of upheaval that means somebody is going away. The middle door of the antique wardrobe, which Lucía opened to get to her clothes, remained open while she packed her bag, so the only thing between Damián and the sounds outside was the thin plywood partition, against which he pressed his ears, alternating them in turn. As he now told Iñaki Gabilondo, whom he'd forced to take up position in the interviewer's seat again, he could hear the hangers rattling and knocking together as Lucía removed her clothes.

"Very faint sounds, I suppose," said the journalist.

"Just imagine it: the hook parts scraping against the pole, metal on metal."

"One might say you were becoming as attuned to sounds as a blind person."

"I didn't have much choice. The annoying thing was not having made myself some kind of peephole; at moments like this, I could have actually seen Lucía in the flesh. I had still only seen her in photos."

The interview with Iñaki Gabilondo was being aired on Canal+, Damián's father's favorite channel. Because it was a subscription channel, the ratings could never match those enjoyed by O'Kane, but it was a more select audience. The set had a restrained look to it, with a table and two chairs against a dark background, and no guests apart from Damián.

"Do you know who Sergio O'Kane is?" Damián said to Gabilondo.

"Sergio O'Kane? I'm afraid not. Should I?"

"Oh, no, probably not. It doesn't matter. I used to be on his show; he used to interview me, but I fired him. He was so vulgar, you see. I'm just moving into a phase of my life where prestige is more important to me than popularity."

"I see," said Gabilondo, his tone evasively neutral.

"What do you think of trashy TV?" Damián now asked.

"To each his own."

"But what do you make of it, trashy TV?"

"What I think," the journalist said severely, "is that I should be the one asking questions."

"I didn't mean to annoy you."

"I'm not annoyed, but there's a rhythm to interviews, and we were just getting somewhere. So anyway, we'd established that you were still in position, in your hiding place in the built-in wardrobe, listening in on the familial commotion that accompanied the preparations for the woman of the house, Lucía, to go away, taking her teenage daughter with her—what did you say her name was?"

"María."

"María. And was there anything else you particularly noticed, aside from these preparations?"

"I noticed something about the way Fede, the husband, was acting. Something neither wife nor daughter picked up on."

"And what was that?"

"He was happy. The prospect of time alone made him happy. Not that he was jumping for joy; on the contrary, everything he did—everything I could make out from the wardrobe anyway—implied that in fact he was sad. He would miss them, he said; if it weren't for the store, he'd be going, too; he really wanted to—all in a whiny sort of tone that just seemed obviously false to me. He didn't mean a word of it, and I knew. It showed me how finely attuned I am when things are being concealed."

"And what did the wife say?"

"The way she was with him . . . It was like she was being overly proper, slightly stiff, which isn't normal if you're married to someone. Like she was holding something back."

"What do you put that down to?"

"The fact she knew that Ghost Butler was listening. She had proof that I was in the house now, and she was keeping up appearances, like she wanted to make it clear that she and her husband weren't cut from the same cloth. I wondered if she might worry that I'd judge her on the basis of her husband's coarseness."

"Is that a way of saying that she preferred you over him?"

"Well, I don't know. Possibly."

ONCE THE FAMILY HAD LEFT the house, Damián climbed out of his hiding place, ate breakfast, performed his ablutions, and wandered a little restlessly from room to room. He had nothing to do, given Lucía's request that he cease all domestic chores while she was away. This enforced inactivity, and the fact it would have to continue until her return, opened up a kind of gap inside him, and a sense of foreboding rushed in. He still had a yearning for glory, and Gabilondo was roundly failing to tick that box. Accustomed as Damián was to huge audiences, these interviews aired on this rarefied channel were deeply unsatisfactory to him.

Why could he not have an internal monologue with himself, as other people presumably did? Why always the necessity for some intermediary when talking to himself about the questions that mattered? Gabilondo now appeared unbidden, asking whether this tendency to talk to himself always via some other person was a kind of depersonalization.

Damián thought for a moment.

"Depersonalization, did you say?"

"Yes, to me it seemed like . . ."

"I don't think that word would ever have occurred to me. But the fact it would never have occurred to me must mean you're the real Gabilondo, and that somehow you've found a way to install yourself in my brain."

"Of course I'm the real Gabilondo; what else could I be? And anyway, you were the one who invited me."

"Yes, because my father says you are a man of

seriousness, and that you're rigorous about your work, in a way no one else is."

"Well, whatever the reason, you asked me here."

"Are you inside other people's heads?"

"Fewer than when I used to have my radio show, but still more than I can reasonably deal with."

Damián Lobo, who was currently in the kitchen, pacing around the table, pulled out a chair and sat down, head in hands.

"When all this started," he said to the journalist, "it was so much simpler."

"And when did it start?"

"It didn't; it's always been this way, ever since I can remember. I remember when I was a schoolkid, I always had some made-up entity alongside me, someone I used to talk to on my way to and from school, recounting my dreams, telling them what had happened in class. I sometimes imagined I was talking to a real-life person, but most of the time it wasn't anyone in particular."

"A kind of imaginary friend?" asked Gabilondo.

"Sort of, but a passive imaginary friend. How can I put it? Someone who only received. Are we filming?"

"I assume so. I always keep the cameras running."

"All right, who cares. . . . Later, when I wasn't

a kid anymore, I gradually started creating this character."

"The person you mentioned before, Sergio O'Kane?"

"Exactly: Sergio O'Kane. The problem was, once I had fleshed him out, he took on a life of his own. Acting of his own accord, doing and saying things that hadn't occurred to me in advance."

"For example?"

"He once induced me, very subtly, to come out against the capitalist system. The auditorium was full to bursting, and people were shaking with laughter. 'The heartlessness of today's capitalism,' he called it. But I'm apolitical, like soccer players."

"And how did you get out of it?"

"I came out with something ambiguous, something I copied from Cristiano Ronaldo."

"I see."

"Since then, I've always found O'Kane hard work."

"In the same way that voices inside a person's head are hard work?"

"What do you mean?"

"I once interviewed a schizophrenic on the radio, and I remember he said the same thing: he found the voices in his head exhausting, mainly because they used to order him to do things that were against his principles."

"Who said anything about schizophrenia?" Damián cut in, clearly annoyed.

"I was telling you about something that happened on my radio show."

"Okay, but watch it. You might be Iñaki Gabilondo, but I can get rid of you if I feel like it, just like I got rid of O'Kane."

"Nobody talks to me like that," Gabilondo said, and promptly vanished.

DAMIÁN LOBO WENT to the computer and typed the word *depersonalization* into the Google search engine. It meant, according to Wikipedia, an unusual way of looking at oneself, as though that self had become separate from one's life or body. It could be caused by sleep deprivation, drug abuse, or prolonged periods of anxiety. Also known as "dissociative disorder," it had the capacity to make the world seem unreal.

None of these symptoms seemed to apply to him, so he closed the Wikipedia page and had a look though the specialist paranormal forums. Ghost Butler remained a sensation, more and more so; it was now rare to find a forum in which he wasn't being discussed. He was a star, and people were signing up to the forums in droves to ask him questions. He always kept his answers short, and tried to stick to the kind of enigmatic utterances people expected of spirits. So when someone asked if death had the effect of putting life's worries into perspective, he replied, "It is surprising how popular the Eiffel Tower is."

A cascade of comments quickly appeared beneath this, offering a slew of interpretations. Ghost Butler, sitting at the computer in María's bedroom, read through them. This was the kind of fame he liked, the kind where the famous person could remain absent. It was completely unlike being on television, especially on public channels, which required you—like the ancient gladiators—to expose yourself to an audience, who would condemn you or reprieve you, in turn, in thrall to instantaneous, fleeting emotions.

He went to point this out to Iñaki Gabilondo but somehow found it impossible to remove himself to the Canal+ studio. A reversal seemed to have taken place: it was no longer that he showed up in the interview, but, rather, that the interview showed up in him. He watched for Gabilondo, he asked him to come, but the journalist took his time, and when finally he did appear, it was as though he had done so of his own volition, not in answer to Damián's call. This is weird, he thought.

"What's weird?" asked Gabilondo, who had read his mind.

"Nothing. I was just having a look at how famous I'm becoming on the internet."

"Outside the internet, as well. One can hardly turn on the television now, or the radio, and not hear mention of Ghost Butler. By the way, what was the Eiffel Tower comment about?"

"Just something that came to me."

"Something a voice inside your head said?"

"No. I told you, it came to me. Fair means, not foul. I don't hear voices."

"Apart from mine, that is."

13

GHOST BUTLER'S DAY was spent on edge, in constant half expectation of Fede's return; with the wife and daughter away, there seemed every chance his routine would change. But in the end, Fede's car pulled into the garage at the normal time; Ghost Butler trotted through to his hiding place and settled down to listen to the sounds in the house. He heard Fede, but he also heard a woman with a shrill voice, who was laughing almost constantly. The pair seemed to do a tour of the house, ending at the master bedroom, where, as Damián had expected, Fede immediately tried to undress the woman. It seemed her name was Paula.

"Easy, tiger," she said, laughing.

"Easy? Why?"

"Give me a minute, okay? It's the first time I've been in your house."

"You're telling me you don't like it here? Better than doing it on packing crates at the store."

"But you sleep with your wife in this bed. What can I say? I don't feel comfortable."

"It's a place like any other. What does it matter if my wife does or doesn't sleep here?"

"You'd have to not be a complete brute to understand."

"I'm a sensitive man. I'm sensitive in my own particular way; I just don't go in for that gushy stereotypical crap. You have to be weak-minded to buy into all that."

"Are you calling me weak-minded, Federico?"

"Are you calling me Federico?"

"I don't want to call you Fede, like your wife does, or your mother, like every other woman in your life. I'm pretty stereotypical in that sense, as well, hon. What I'd like would be for us to have our very own private language. For you to talk to me in a way you never have to anyone else."

"*Jalapa sela visterra mare.*"

"*Sorni vinilo dernala puore.*"

Fede and the woman both began laughing.

"Which of the two of us," she said, "do you think could keep that up for the longest?"

"You," he said.

"Why?"

"Because you care more about the way words sound than what they mean."

"What I care about is what actions mean. I'm not at all comfortable, for instance, lying down on the bed you sleep in with your wife."

"Here we go again."

"It must be my weak-mindedness—but you like weak-minded women, don't you, Federico?"

"I love it when you turn into a complete airhead."

"All men love airheads."

"Right on, and that's one stereotype I definitely fit. Go on, shake that ass for me."

"First of all, tell me which side your wife sleeps on."

"This one."

"Okay, you're going there, then. Then I get to feel like I'm fucking you and your wife at the same time. . . ."

"You're starting to wind me up."

"*Vondrila mixta culosa repe.*"

"What we're going to do is imagine this is a hotel. Room service and everything."

"What if she turns up?"

"How's she going to turn up if she's on the other side of the country?"

"Some people are able to be in two places at once. In fact, I can feel her presence here. But seriously, let's pause on that; it's turning me on. You said she'd gone to see her sick mother?"

"Yes."

"Okay, so imagine her mom dying while you and I are lying here, together in her bed, fucking like animals, and she dies at the exact moment we come."

Fede burst out laughing, ramping up the sexual tension; then silence ensued as the pair fell to kissing. Ghost Butler guessed that Paula was an employee at the toy store, and was a good deal younger than both Lucía and Fede.

It was all too easy imagining their maneuvers: him on the attack, her fending him off, trying to go back to talking. From what Damián could ascertain, there were intervals of kissing in the bed, followed by the pair disentangling, standing up, and resuming verbal foreplay. Though Ghost Butler's poor diet had undoubtedly resulted in some loss of vitality, he was becoming moderately aroused, though not to the extent that he wanted to masturbate.

"All those games turned me on," said Damián, as if he were being interviewed in a television studio, but the studio wasn't there, nor an interviewer, nor an imaginary friend: nothing at all. He was talking to nothing and to no one, and it continued that way for some time, until, seemingly at random, Iñaki Gabilondo appeared inside his head.

"You took your time!" exclaimed Ghost Butler.

"Like to fill me in?" asked the journalist.

"Fede has brought a woman back—I think she works at the toy store with him—and they're going at it like rabbits."

"Well, well. I never had you down as a Peeping Tom."

"I wasn't peeping, just listening."

"Listening is a form of watching."

"I was listening to them moaning and groaning."

"I'm not prepared to discuss such things on my program," said Gabilondo.

"That's because you think you're above trash TV, like my father does. If this was Sergio O'Kane's show, we'd be going viral by now."

"Well, you are very welcome to return to that show," said Gabilondo, once more absenting himself from Damián's mental space.

But when Sergio O'Kane failed to heed his call, Ghost Butler succumbed to an anxiety attack, which he then tried to combat with a blow-by-blow account of the couple in bed, his inner monologue devolving into a rapid sports commentary–like patter. It was, he realized, a way of keeping his mind busy as well as tiring himself out physically. Indeed, when the raucous sounds—more akin to two people murdering each other than making love—reached the crescendo of a simultaneous orgasm, Damián went slack all over, as though he had been joining in.

Since the lovers' words, resumed now after a few moments of silence, were being whispered rather than spoken, Ghost Butler decided to risk opening the makeshift door connecting the built-in wardrobe to the old wooden one, so that he could hear what they were saying.

"What was that?" said Fede, hearing a noise in the wardrobe. (The ghost's head had hit an empty clothes hanger, nearly knocking it down.)

"What?" said Paula. "I didn't hear anything."

"Are you sure?"

"Yeah. Where?"

"There, in the wardrobe."

"A ghost, probably. Or your wife's employed a private detective."

"A detective, that's a pretty outlandish idea—but a ghost, maybe. Lucía believes in ghosts. I'm going to take a look."

"Oh, come on, just when we were getting cozy.

Stay. Didn't you say she was on the other side of the country?"

Ghost Butler held his breath and stood rigid, not daring to pull his head back in, for fear of making more noise. In the end, Fede stayed where he was, and the lovers turned to mockery of Lucía.

"Isn't that wardrobe ugly?" said the man.

"As sin. Looks like it's off the set of a horror movie. Or from a funeral parlor."

"Lucía happened on it in an antiques market—amazing, really: it belonged to her grandparents. They lived in a village near Santander, in a house where she spent part of her childhood. She recognized it from some marks on the right side—you know, the kind parents make to record their children's heights at different ages. I'll show you."

"What a crazy coincidence."

"And she went ahead and bought the damn thing without asking me. Then she goes and sticks it there—there's a built-in wardrobe right behind it, it's huge, and now we can't get to it. So it's like we've got this kind of gulag behind there. If you ever feel like kidnapping someone, you know where to bring them."

"Your wife's kind of crazy, right?"

"She has her moments."

"Didn't you tell me she's missing a finger?"

"Yes, the forefinger on her right hand. And this was the very wardrobe she shut it in, the middle door."

"The whole thing's so hot. . . . A lady with a missing finger, that's hot; the spooky wardrobe, that's hot; you lying where your wife normally lies, hot; you being called Federico, that, too. . . ."

"*Servila valium pirtera enganya.*"

"Don't, don't, you'll get me going again. Hold on, here; touch me just here."

"With what?"

"With your wife's missing finger."

As the lovers embraced once more, and as the volume levels rose, Ghost Butler slipped back inside the built-in wardrobe. He was exhausted. He felt his way down onto his berth, curled up in the fetal position, and closed his eyes. His thoughts were filled with ideas about the world, about life, and how both were bursting with strange moments like the one he had just over-heard, all of it perfect material, he thought, for a book that could be called *The Life of Insects*. He did not know why, but the behavior of Fede and Paula seemed to him more like that of insects than the kind of thing mammals got up to. A pic-ture of Lucía's hand came into his head, and as he considered the stub where the right forefinger would once have been, an enormous, infinite sensation of tenderness washed over him; he imagined taking that hand and holding it to his chest, thereby protecting the other fingers. Thinking these things, he was soon asleep.

14

THE RADIO-ALARM came on at the regular time, and with the usual burst of distressing information (a young couple had died in Alcorcón after their gas heater leaked). The news affected the ghost more than it did the lovers, who, the instant they awoke, immediately began refamiliarizing themselves with each other's bodies—as though each had acquired a new body in the night and they needed to reacquaint themselves. Their explorations went on for twenty minutes, the cries of pain and pleasure combining with complaints from Fede in particular that he was going to be late.

The young woman, Paula, got out of the bed a little sleepily and came over to the antique wardrobe, throwing open one of the doors and peering inside, remarking on how surprisingly spacious it was. She must, Damián thought, have had her head right inside the wardrobe as she made some of these remarks, given the way her voice seemed to bounce around the interior, as though in a cathedral. She closed the door and called out to Fede that it smelled awful in there.

"Like old chicken shit," said Fede, also at a shout, from the bathroom. "It was used as a chicken coop at one point."

The woman said something in return, which Damián only half-heard, about the mental health of her lover's wife, and the noises from outside became those of any regular couple preparing for the day ahead. To mitigate their lateness after lying in bed so long, they skipped breakfast, so Damián heard the garage door slam at about the same time it did on the days the family left together.

Ghost Butler gave it a short while, as was his custom, in case anything had been forgotten and someone were to reappear. Then he climbed out of the built-in wardrobe, through the three-part one, and appeared in the bedroom, his movements supple and somewhat undulating, as though he were made of smoke. The room was an appalling mess. The bedspread lay in a heap on the floor—it looked as though the lovers had walked back and forth across it—and the crumpled sheets gave off a chlorine- or bleachlike smell, signifying semen, which Damián found disgusting. It was the same in the bathroom, where he found numerous long copper-colored hairs in the sink, presumably Paula's, along with a few smears of toothpaste, like the excrement of some milky white worm. The towels had been used and dumped on the bidet, and whoever had used the toilet last had neglected to flush it.

Damián left everything as it was, knowing he needed to remain inconspicuous, and went to María's bathroom to wash. Making his way into the kitchen, he found dirty cups and plates strewn across the countertops, and items taken out of the fridge and not put back. He stood surveying the scene, wondering despondently how long he could cope with such untidiness, when he noticed a cell phone charger plugged in by the microwave. One of the lovers must have forgotten it. Looking more closely, he saw it was the same brand as his cell phone.

This was interesting. Having weaned himself off the world at large, he was now faced with an opportunity to charge his cell phone and call his sister or father, and thereby establish if they were still alive, and if either had reported him missing. He had occasionally felt drawn to picking up the landline phone in the house to contact one of them, but he knew the number would come up on the phone of whomever he did call, and that could be used as evidence against him further down the line.

He had avoided going out in the garden for

similar reasons; there might be security cameras in the streets of the housing development, or perhaps he'd be photographed by one of the many satellites orbiting the planet. He had come into the house inside a wardrobe, and he could only leave in some similar fashion. Inside a coffin? he thought somberly.

In any event, the idea of either quitting the house or being removed from it—which came to him on a semiregular basis—brought with it a feeling of deep distress. The outside world was alien to him now. His detachment from it was total.

And so he went and found his cell phone, plugged it into the forgotten charger, and, after picking halfheartedly at some breakfast, went into María's room to surf the net for a while. It turned out that on the paranormal forums his periods of silence were being scrutinized with no less intensity than any comments he had made.

"The Ghost Butler's silences," wrote one forum user, "are filled with voices."

"Emptinesses are always full," he wrote in reply to this comment, for want of anything better to say. This instigated an immediate deluge of further comments.

He soon logged out of that forum, having only wished to check if Lucía might have found some

coverage and be online. He was looking up information on anorexia and menstruation when suddenly, while still sitting at María's computer, he
found himself in Iñaki Gabilondo's television
studio.

"What are you up to?" the journalist asked.

"Oh," said Damián, "seeing if I can get to the
bottom of whatever it is María's experiencing—the
teenage daughter in the house. She still hasn't gotten her period. I think it's something to do with her
eating problems. If I'm going to be the one taking
care of her from now on, I want to try to understand what she's going through."

"You're thinking of adopting?" Gabilondo asked.

"In a way, I've already adopted the whole family."

"Did you know how well our last few interviews
have gone down with viewers?" Gabilondo said,
abruptly changing the subject.

"Have you got viewing figures?"

"On a subscription channel like this, we don't
worry so much about the numbers as the caliber of
our viewership. Our subscribers have been shown
to be almost exclusively university graduates and
highly qualified white-collar workers. In other
words, the tastemakers, the people who tell the
rest of society what to think."

At this, Gabilondo turned to one of the cameras,

bestowing on it a look of either recognition or thanks.

"We've had all kinds of people calling in about you," he continued. "Wanting to know about your current situation, of course, asking about the reasons behind your social exclusion, but also inquiring as to the peculiar class of alienation, one of the unmistakable defining characteristics of the capitalist system, that has led you to become such a star of the small screen."

"You've got a bee in your bonnet about capitalism, as well?"

"I see my role as that of a witness to the state of the world as it truly is. In the eyes of any sociologist, you clearly exhibit some of the pathologies associated with alienation."

"Alienation?"

"That's what people say when they want to refer to the process that, within certain economic systems, makes it impossible for people to construct an identity for themselves."

"But it is possible to take on someone else's?"

"Precisely. That is precisely what we're talking about. Becoming someone else."

"Is that the 'depersonalization' thing, the 'dissociative disorder' you were talking about the other day?"

"In a sense, yes."

"I looked it up on Wikipedia. Didn't sound like me."

"The alienated individual is unaware of his or her own othering. Hence the resounding success of the economic and political systems whose main supporter base is their own victims."

"Are you a Communist, Iñaki?"

"Remember, it's me who asks the questions here."

"Sure, you ask, I answer. And what I always say is that I don't answer political questions. I don't take sides. In that way, you could think of me as being like a celebrity chef or a soccer player. I've got fans who vote left, right, and somewhere in the middle, the whole political spectrum. And it's important I respect them all. I have no choice but to be neutral in such matters."

"But, given your presence as a public figure, you presumably won't mind if we change tack a little and ask about your private life."

"You're going to have to wait. I need to look at the messages on my cell phone; I've just been charging it up."

While remaining in the studio, Damián Lobo took himself physically into the kitchen, turned on the cell phone, which had a full charge now, and scrolled through the messages. There were some thirty or forty, all promotions and advertisements except for one: a missed call from his sister.

"Just calling my sister," he said to the journalist. "To ask how everything's going out there."

"No hurry."

His sister answered, and gave no indication she was surprised at Damián's lengthy absence.

"You must be wondering why I haven't called in such a long time," he said.

"No, actually," said the sister. "I thought you'd gone to Alicante."

"Why Alicante?" he asked.

"I'm not sure. I remember thinking, My brother hasn't called. And then the idea of Alicante came into my head."

The siblings spoke briefly before Damián returned to the studio to pass on the news that his family was all right, and that his father had used the entirety of his savings, including a substantial pension plan, to buy his Chinese sister a gift store in the Salamanca neighborhood of Madrid, a store that she was now running.

"A high-quality gift store," he added. "Like the Canal+ of gift stores. She said it's going really well."

"But your parents aren't Chinese—or are they?" Gabilondo asked.

"Not them, my sister."

Speaking into one of the cameras now, Damián recounted his family history; how his parents, two or three years after they married, and finding themselves still childless, adopted a Chinese baby, traveling to an orphanage in that far-off country to collect her in person.

"The truth is," he said, "from what I've been able to work out, they bought her."

"How old was she?" the journalist asked.

"A few months," said Damián.

"Why didn't they want a Spanish baby?"

"Spain's purchasing power was good at the time, and it was fashionable to give money to Third World causes."

"But China's the second-greatest global power."

"Maybe not at the time. I don't know. It was the kind of thing people thought well of."

He then explained how, two years after the adoption, and though the parents had not been trying, he was conceived.

"They hadn't been planning on another baby; all their parental urges had been satisfied with the one child, so when I came along, they treated me like the adopted one."

"They treated you badly?" Gabilondo asked.

"More like they were always doing me a favor.

Like they'd saved me from an orphanage. My Chinese sister was this incredibly charming little girl, uncommonly so, whereas I was withdrawn, sullen even. I felt like I was the one who'd come into the family unit from outside, from some far-off place."

"Let's just pause there," Gabilondo said. "Could you go into a little more detail about that?"

"I sometimes feel like they loved my sister more because they'd spent money getting her."

"A classic trait of those inside the capitalist system."

"You guys are obsessed!"

"Sorry, but you said it. Anyway, go on, please."

"My parents brought in a Chinese maid, saying they wanted my sister to have some reflection of herself around the house. They worried about her being the only Chinese person in our orbit, that her singular appearance would be an obstacle in the socializing process. But I was the one who spent hours and hours in the kitchen with the Chinese maid, and I was the one who developed a closeness with her. My sister conducted herself like a normal Spanish person, while I felt Chinese, more and more so as the years passed. I spent a lot of time looking in the mirror, squinting, trying to make my eyes look like those of the maid, who, by the

way, loved me like her own child. She once told me
I was like the child she'd never had."

"And what was she to you?"

"The same: like the mother I hadn't had. But
when my parents noticed the bond between us,
they fired her. That hit me pretty hard."

"Did the two of you stay in touch at all?"

"A bit. She found ways to carry on seeing me.
She would come to my school at recess and stand
at the fence, looking in. She handed me little notes,
messages saying she loved me; I've still got them.
On Mother's Day, I'd draw pictures of dragons for
her."

"All without your mother and father finding
out?"

"Yes, they never knew."

"Are you still in touch with her?"

"We haven't talked in a while, but I have her
address and her number. She doesn't work anymore; she's quite old. She lives in a shared house in
Usera, quite near to me, and I go visit sometimes."

"Perhaps we could bring her on the show one
day."

"Perhaps."

"Are those tears? Are you crying?"

"I find it quite emotional talking about her."

"What's her name?"

"Ai. Which, as it happens, means 'love.'"

"And what's your Chinese sister's name?"

"Desirée, which means 'beloved.'"

Damián knew tears were great for ratings, even on a subscription channel, but he did what he could to stem them, knowing also that these kinds of viewers prized emotional control above disinhibition, which also explained Gabilondo's decision not to delve into the subject any further.

"If you'll excuse me," said Damián, getting up from his chair, "I've got some things I need to do."

"Please," said the journalist.

15

FEDE, TOGETHER with his lover, Paula, came back to the house late in the afternoon, and the pair wasted no time in proceeding to the bedroom. As the previous day's amorous games recommenced, like a repeated gymnastics sequence, Damián, lying on his back inside the cave, staring up into the darkness with fingers interlaced behind his neck, experienced a blinding flash inside his head, followed by an overwhelming sense of calm—a combination that told him everything was in order. He immediately passed this on to Gabilondo.

"There's just been an explosion of light inside my head."

"You sure you didn't have a stroke?" the journalist asked with a smirk.

"No, not a stroke. The kind of thunderbolt that lights up a dark room, illuminating everything, showing you where the table is, the chairs, the cupboard—everything set out in an unworldly kind of order. The way my brain lit up was exactly like that, and I saw all my ideas finally fall into place."

"Sounds like a mystical moment," Gabilondo said—still a little ironically, though Damián gave no sign of noticing.

"Call it what you like. The point is that I have just been shown, without a shadow of a doubt, that I've found my place in the world."

"Your place in the world is inside the built-in wardrobe?"

"The built-in wardrobe, but also this studio; they are both my place, and I can occupy both at the same time. Like the way two people can be thinking the same thing at once."

"Do you think you're a thought?"

"Of course. I'm closer to being a thought than a flesh-and-blood human being."

"But are Fede and Paula still fucking?" the journalist said, cutting Damián off.

This took Damián aback: it was more O'Kane's style than the kind of question he'd associate with Gabilondo.

"So your subscription-only viewers like cheap sex, too, do they?" he asked knowingly.

Gabilondo cleared his throat, with the air of a person caught red-handed. For a moment, Damián glimpsed a few flecks of yellow in his eyes: they were just like O'Kane's. Sergio O'Kane's spirit had apparently taken up residence inside the well-respected journalist's body.

"It's you, Sergio," Damián protested. "I see you!"

"But in a different embodiment," said O'Kane. "Don't worry about it—appearances are everything."

Damián weighed the situation. He liked the prestige of being interviewed by Gabilondo, but he missed the feeling of popularity that came with being on O'Kane's show. Perhaps his dilemma had in fact been solved: the body of the former, invested with the latter's way of thinking.

"What should I call you now? Sergio Gabilondo or Iñaki O'Kane?"

"Let's go with Iñaki O'Kane. I've always liked my surname more than my first name. But back to what I was saying: Are Fede and Paula still going at it?"

Fede and Paula had indeed been continuing their gymnastics routine, though they must have just executed the final maneuver, Damián thought, and be lying spent, because it had been absolutely silent in the room for a number of minutes now.

"Absolute silence," Damián Lobo said to O'Kane, "experienced in a place of absolute darkness: nothing feels more like death."

"Did you have the sensation of being dead?"

"Exactly that. Then I put my ear to the panel, and thought I could hear Fede snoring."

"And then?"

"Lithe and supple as a ghost, I slipped into the antique wardrobe, and, pausing to check all was still quiet, I pushed lightly on the middle door, which gave a slight creak. Again I let a few moments elapse before poking my head out, to find the lovers lying naked on the bed. They were in such a deep sleep that I tiptoed daringly over to the bed for a closer look. She had a face that was what you might almost call overstated: big bulging eyes, big nose, thick lips—Botox, possibly— wide forehead. . . ."

"And her body?"

"The same: large breasts, big hips, tiny about the waist."

"Pretty attractive, it sounds like?"

"But a rather unrefined sort of attractiveness. Not the Canal+ kind."

Iñaki O'Kane must have received a message in his earpiece.

"Take your time," O'Kane replied, addressing an indeterminate point in the space, "that's the good thing about doing a prerecord. It all gets edited later on, so we can always cut things if we want."

Damián, meanwhile, took a moment to inspect Fede's features, which, unlike the woman's, were sort of vague. Like they're being erased, he said to himself. The face seemed to him half-formed, embryonic: nascent eyes, nascent nose, nascent (gaping) mouth. Something of the fetus floating in the protective fluids of sleep. The pair's clothes, scattered on the floor around the bed, gave the scene a disorderly air, which the ghost found aggravating. It was just about to climb back into its hiding place, but on an impulse, it scooped up the young woman's panties and took them inside.

WHEN THE LOVERS AWOKE, a couple of hours later, Fede used the phone on the bedside table to order in pizza. When the takeout arrived, they ate it in bed, washed down with a beer each, joking all the while about the situation they found themselves in.

"Can you imagine if your wife saw us now?" asked Paula.

"She'd be horrified—the house is a mess."

"And what would horrify her more? You and me devouring each other, or us eating pizza in bed?"

"Oh, the pizza, for sure. I told you she's pretty much frigid."

"How long has it been since the two of you last fucked?"

"Man, not since before the wardrobe came."

"You talk about the before and after of that wardrobe arriving like it's the before and after of the birth of Christ."

"That's because there was a before and an after. It wasn't that wonderful before, but since then, it's been all kinds of shitty. It is all kinds of shitty. Honestly, I've had enough."

"Why did you marry her?"

"Beats me. A genuine mystery. My parents died when I was young, and hers kind of took me in. It was them I liked being with, more than I ever did her. They gave me the money to set up the store. Then the father—he was the one I got on best with— died, and the mother went to live in Santander, at Lucía's grandparents' house. The place the wardrobe came from."

"My parents would love you, too," said Paula with a suggestive titter. "They're very loving, and they're both still alive."

"They must be getting that bed in a terrible state," Damián said to Iñaki O'Kane.

"Well, you shouldn't worry about that. Know how many new subscriptions Canal+ has registered since it started airing your interviews?"

"No idea."

"Twenty thousand, in barely more than four days."

"And how many have canceled their subscriptions?"

"The loss rate has stayed at its usual level."

"I bet my father's one of the ones who's canceled."

"Do you care?"

"I don't know. I always wanted Canal+ viewers to like me, but children do take too long to fulfill their parents' wishes. Could you do me a favor, O'Kane?"

"Sure."

"Put some colored contacts in? To hide the yellow in your eyes? It's the one thing giving away the fact you aren't Iñaki Gabilondo."

"I'll do it for you. And for your father."

16

AFTER FINISHING the pizzas and beer, Fede and Paula probably fell asleep in each other's arms, like lovers in the movies: her head on his chest, and their legs entwined like the roots of two adjacent plants. So Damián imagined, as their voices grew quiet, until eventually he could barely make out their words. In view of this, he had no choice but to abandon the built-in wardrobe, taking all the care in the world, and assume a position inside the antique wardrobe; it wasn't easy to arrange himself both comfortably and in such a way that he would be able to slide quickly back into his hiding place if the need arose. When he was finally able to put his ear to the door, Fede was telling Paula the story of how he and Lucía had met:

" . . . in a hospital, strangely enough. We'd been admitted around the same time, both with wasp stings; we're both allergic. It was pretty serious; we both nearly died. Your throat closes up, you know; there's a point when you can't breathe. Anyway, when I got better, one of the nurses asked me to stop by the bed of a young woman who was in another ward, to go and cheer her up. That young woman turned out to be Lucía."

"How many wasps had you each been stung by?"

"Just one each, but if you're allergic, that's all it takes. Just pray the ambulance doesn't take too long."

A silence followed, broken after a few moments by Paula.

"So all it would take to finish your wife off would be one itsy wasp sting?"

"Probably not, actually—we both always keep the antidote at hand." Fede paused for a moment. "Anyway, what are you trying to say?"

"Exactly what you're thinking, my love."

"Don't be dumb."

"Let's see," she said, persisting. "Imagine being able to kill your wife just by thinking it. I wish my wife was dead, you think, and she's dead."

At that moment, the phone on the bedside table rang, and Fede picked it up. It was Lucía, asking how everything was. Fine, fine, Fede said; he was planning on an early night, since he needed to be at the store early; he was halfway through doing an inventory. Damián recounted all of this, more or less in real time, to Iñaki O'Kane, who for his part seemed to have come to terms with the relative frostiness of his new environment, where the sparse Canal+ audience reacted stony-faced to his every utterance.

"And what did Paula do?" the interviewer asked.

"Held her breath, I think," said Damián. "I'm fairly certain she wouldn't have moved a muscle, not wanting Lucía to twig."

And indeed, the only sound to be heard was the voice of Fede, who managed to stay remarkably calm. He asked after Lucía's mother, and after María, and there can't have been much news, because he immediately made an excuse—he had something in the oven, he said—and signed off. Hanging up, he breathed a loud sigh of relief, to Paula's amusement.

"You sounded stiff as hell," she said. "She must know something's up."

"What do you mean? I didn't sound natural?"

"As natural as someone can be who's talking on the phone to his wife while his bit on the side is lying in the bed next to him—buck naked."

"Okay. . . . And what were you saying before, about wishing her dead?"

"Oh, just that: that if you were able to kill her just by thinking it, would you?"

"I'm going to have to think about that. . . ."

"Don't tell me you haven't before, a thousand times."

"Sure, but not seriously. Not like I actually wanted it to happen. I'm guessing you have?"

"All the time. Problem is, they never play ball, the assholes."

"Right. People don't just drop dead. Something has to happen to them."

"Oh, I just remembered something!" said Paula.

"I'm all ears."

"A story I read in the paper last summer, about a guy, from Asturias, I think, who died after taking out the trash. A trash bag had been left in the garden overnight, and it had food scraps in it, and a whole load of wasps had gotten inside. When he picked it up, they swarmed out at him, and they were pissed as hell. He was allergic, and didn't make it to the hospital in time."

"If you're a guy who's allergic to wasps, and you walk straight into a nest, it's all over."

"And if you're a girl?"

"As in?"

"What happens if you're a girl who's allergic to wasps?"

"What do you think? Exactly the same."

"Well, that's that, then, isn't it?"

"What's what?"

"Oh, come on, don't play dumb."

"You're wrong in the head, babe."

"Come *on*." She laughed. "It's the time of year when the wasps start coming out. Say the word and I'll collect a bunch for you, and when I've got say twenty or thirty, I'll hand them over, you put them inside a trash bag, don't tie it up properly, and then tell Lucía to go take out the trash."

"It's my job to take out the trash."

"So tell her you're feeling sick."

The pair fell silent for a few moments, and Damián was considering a return to his hiding place, when Fede spoke again.

"Christ," he said. "You had me worried for a moment there. I thought you meant it."

"Well," she said, "a whole lot of crimes start like this, as a joke. Just you wait: the wife-murdering-wasp idea is in your head now, and it won't go away."

"I mean, the thought's occurred to me before, but until you actually talk to someone about something, it doesn't seem real."

"Hold on! I *was* joking. You won't catch me going wasp gathering anytime soon. What you need to do is end the relationship."

"Then what?"

"Sell the toy store, and we set up a franchise."

"What kind of franchise?"

"A Starbucks. Do you know how much it costs to make a cup of coffee, and how much they sell them for?"

"O-*kay*. So I'll tell you what we *are* going to do: clean the kitchen up a bit—Lucía's been away just two days, and you've seen what it's like in there—then you're going to help me shake the bed out; there're crumbs everywhere."

"Ha! You feel like cleaning now because the grubby idea of bumping your wife off has gotten inside your head."

Damián sensed them getting out of the bed, and he made to withdraw, but then, realizing how hard it would be to move swiftly but silently, he decided to stay put.

"I can't find my panties," said Paula, her voice seemingly inches from the wardrobe.

"Is this another joke?"

"No! What did you do with them?"

"What do you mean, what did I do with them?"

"It was you who took them off."

They were both quiet a moment as Fede presumably cast about for the panties.

"I don't get it," he said. "I took them off you, and

I tossed them over the side of the bed. . . . They've got to be here somewhere."

"Fine, but I wouldn't want to be around when Lucía finds them."

"Good thing she's got some exactly the same."

"What do you mean, she's got some exactly the same? *You* gave those to me as a present! Do you like me and her wearing the same lingerie?"

Fede was clearly stumped.

"Um . . ." he said eventually, "she bought an identical pair for herself after I bought you these ones. They're from the lingerie store at the mall. . . ."

"Are you sure?"

"Totally. What do you take me for?"

The voices moved around the space while the pair continued to argue, from which Damián surmised they were still hunting for the panties.

"It drives me nuts when things go astray like this," said Fede. "When there's just no reason for it."

"Go astray? I don't think so. They've been lost. Going astray is like losing your way. Why'd you call it that?"

"Goddammit, I don't know. I'm losing my mind over here, first the wasps, now the panties. Plus Lucía calling on the phone. I'm starting to feel pretty weird."

"Well, come take a look at this. Don't I look good in this old antique mirror?"

Damián pictured the woman posing in the wardrobe mirror. Then he heard laughter, as though perhaps Fede had come up behind her and was hugging and tickling her at the same time. And indeed, another gymnastics routine followed, with the two returning to bed for a time. When it was over, judging by the quiet that once more enveloped the room, they again fell asleep. Damián strained to listen, and presently picked out Fede's gentle snoring, all too familiar by now. He ducked into the built-in wardrobe, brought out the panties, and, opening the middle door of the antique wardrobe a ways, flung them into the room.

"I shouldn't have taken them in the first place," he said to Iñaki O'Kane.

"Why did you?"

"I don't know. An impulse, I guess, a fetish."

The panties sailing through the air must have created a draft, because Fede woke up.

"What was that?" he said.

"What?" Paula said sleepily.

"I don't know. Did you say something?"

"I was dreaming away, lover."

"We were going to clean the kitchen," he said.

"Don't sweat it. I'll get up early tomorrow and do it. When's the woman of the house coming back?"

"Not yet."

Fede must have gotten out of the bed, because there then came a cry.

"Your panties!"

"What's up now?"

"They're here. Look!"

"But we looked there. . . ."

"I know."

"Well, all I can say is, either you're messing with my head or I'm messing with yours."

WHEN THE LOVERS DISAPPEARED into the kitchen, Damián Lobo slid out of the antique wardrobe and into his cave, where, following this small effort, he found himself bathed in sweat; it felt as though he were dissolving in it, like a bar of soap under a tap. He undressed down to his boxers and lay on his back before patting and prodding his body, pausing and probing at its various regions like someone tuning an instrument.

"I'm turning into a fakir," he said to himself—Iñaki O'Kane seemed not to be in residence.

Running his fingers through his long beard, he

was once more put in mind of Robinson Crusoe as depicted in an illustrated volume he remembered from his childhood home. He thought of himself as a shipwreck who'd washed up in that wardrobe, just as Robinson Crusoe had on his island. Perhaps, he thought, he ought to have marked the passing of the days since his shipwreck with notches on the wardrobe panels. He tried to work out how long he had been there, but the days all melded into one, making it impossible. There was no longer any such thing as time. He thought of it as a kind of conditioned reflex from his former life. He then heard Iñaki O'Kane's voice saying that Damián had, in some way, installed himself in eternity.

"In eternity?" Damián said, confused.

"Well," said O'Kane, "one of the possible versions of eternity."

IT WAS LATE WHEN Fede and Paula came back to the bedroom; perhaps they had been watching television. One and then the other used the bathroom, to judge by the to-ing and fro-ing of their voices.

"And what about María?" Fede said.

"Which María?"

"Which María do you think? My daughter."

"I don't follow. 'What about María' what?"

"If Lucía were to die."

"Can't leave it alone now, can you?"

"It was you who brought it up."

"Oh, come on, only in a speculative way."

"Fine, just speculatively, then: What would happen to María?"

"I'd make a perfect stepmom. I get on great with teenagers. Also, I happen to think she's a wonderful girl; she's got a lot going for her."

"I haven't told you, but she's been having eating problems."

"Just like me at her age."

"And she hasn't gotten her period yet."

"I didn't start until I was sixteen; it just depends."

"She's been pretending she has started, buying tampons and then soaking them in red ink. We've kind of just played along."

"Come on, she's the one playing along with you guys."

A silence now followed while, Damián surmised, they got into bed. After a few moments, Paula spoke again.

"How long have you lived in this house?"

"Going on a year," Fede said. "Why?"

"Because it's got its own particular smell. All houses do. It depends on the personality of the family living in them."

"I can't really tell."

"That's because you smell it every single day. Like smokers who don't notice how they smell."

"And what does this house smell of?"

"I don't know, off milk?"

"Like yogurt?"

"I said off milk."

"Off milk sounds pretty disgusting."

"Don't take it the wrong way; it's very faint. It's kind of like a smell from childhood; I can't pin it down exactly, though. Take a real deep breath. Can you really not smell that?"

"No, I'm getting nothing."

Damián thought she must be referring to him, to the smell that he, the ghost, had been producing as he sloughed off his physical form. He felt like airing the idea with O'Kane, but O'Kane was still nowhere to be found. Outside the wardrobe, Fede had turned on the radio, which was playing the nightly sports show.

Damián was about to go to sleep when some images came into his head that he had seen on the internet while looking up information on late-onset menstruation. On Wikipedia, the fallopian tubes were also referred to as "uterine tubes, leading from the ovaries to the womb." At first glance, he'd read this as "leading from the ovaries to the tomb," the idea of which made him feel quite uneasy. He had inspected the image of the ovaries, in which the eggs are produced, and which are connected to the uterus by the fallopian tubes. As he drifted toward sleep, he saw the reproductive organs before him, with the egg, or ovum, traveling along the fallopian tubes, or oviducts, over a period of twenty-four to forty-eight hours; it pauses there, hoping the sperm will come and meet it. If the sperm fails to show up on time, the egg continues on its way, eventually to be shed through the vagina. At the point when the egg left the woman's body, Damián gave a shudder. But by then he was already asleep.

17

THE NEXT DAY, hearing Fede and Paula leave for the toy store, Damián climbed out of his cave, though in one sense he stayed exactly where he was; anyplace he now passed through, he had begun also to linger in, as though he had attained a certain degree of omnipresence. He went down the hall, holding up his sweatpants with his hands, for though he had tightened the drawstring as much as possible, they kept falling down. Taking a seat at the kitchen table, still littered with dirty plates and half-eaten things—Fede and the woman had not followed through on the previous night's discussion and cleaned up—he spent a number of minutes contemplating the idea that, for all he believed himself to be there, he was not there and had actually remained in the wardrobe. Sleep and wakefulness had become indistinguishable to him in texture. He was no longer quite sure whether he had stayed asleep or gotten up, or whether he was still inside his hiding place, or elsewhere.

"Is this really happening?" he asked Iñaki O'Kane, trusting that his question would travel to wherever the hybrid journalist might be.

"It's starting to happen," came O'Kane's instant reply.

This time, Damián did not find himself inside the television studio, nor did the yellow-eyed face appear before him; there was only the interviewer's voice, clear as a bell, somewhere inside his head.

"What's starting to happen?" Damián asked.

"You've found out how to do away with Fede: wasps."

"Are you telling me what to do?" Damián said.

"Take it however you want," said the voice. "Just be sure to act."

"Listen here, O'Kane," said Damián, "you're a figment of *my* imagination."

"And now I'm reimagining you," the interviewer said. "That way, we'll be even."

Damián thought about this for a few minutes. Nothing made sense. He was reminded of a show he had seen on television as a child. It had featured a run-of-the-mill ventriloquist with a dummy, also entirely run-of-the-mill. The amazing moment had been when they opened their mouths, and it became apparent that the dummy was the ventriloquist, and the ventriloquist his dummy.

He made himself a cup of milky tea and went through into María's bedroom, turning on the computer and navigating to the forums on paranormal activity. He had received no word from Lucía, but it was noticeable how many of the other forum users had been clamoring for him to weigh in. One of them had posted a message, asking how you were supposed to tell if a house was haunted.

"There will be a faint smell of off milk," Damián wrote.

He signed out of the forum, and typed in the following question: "What do wasps eat?"

He learned that their preference was for sugar- and protein-based foods, though in fact there was little they refused to eat—hence their willingness to forage in people's trash. An article came up describing how to make a trap using a two-liter soda bottle. The idea was to cut off the top, just below the neck, then flip the top portion upside down and insert it into the bottle to create a funnel, with the narrow bit pointing downward to the lower part, which you'd previously filled with your chosen bait. The wasps would smell the bait and fly in, but they wouldn't be able to find their way out again. It seemed so easy that he immediately looked up whether someone with an allergy really could die from a single sting; the answer was yes.

In under an hour, the victim's ears would swell up, along with the person's throat, tongue, lips, and glottis, causing breathing difficulties and an acute drop in arterial pressure. These were the symptoms one could expect if someone went into anaphylactic shock.

He deleted his search history, taking even more care this time than usual, turned off the computer, and went into the garage, where, as luck would have it, the family kept multipacks of bottled water, which they tended to drink instead of tap water. He gathered five bottles into his arms, went back to the kitchen, and poured the contents down the sink. Then, following the instructions he had read online, he placed a few slivers of cooked ham in the lower portion of each bottle before creeping out into the garden as stealthily as he was able. He had forgotten neither the prying neighbors nor the satellites with their ultra-long-range cameras. He positioned the traps where he'd be able to see them from the window and then went back inside. The wasps were slower to arrive than expected, but once one or two had found the bottles, substantial numbers soon followed. Within a half hour, a small, shifting cloud had gathered over each of the traps, and the wasps began finding their way to the scraps of ham. Come midday, some thirty wasps had fallen into the five bottles.

The challenge now was to transfer the wasps to the trash can in the kitchen. He went online again, where he learned they could be stunned with the use of smoke, and furthermore that it was easy to make a kind of torch using aluminum foil and newspaper. If you made a cone from the aluminum foil and filled it with crumpled pieces of newspaper, then put a match to the pointed part of the cone, the pulp inside the paper would heat up, producing copious amounts of smoke.

He worked in the kitchen sink to make any surplus easier to clean up. Just as the internet article had suggested, the aluminum cone became a kind of little smoke barrel; lighting it, he went around the traps in turn, inverting them and holding the tops over the rising smoke. The wasps were rendered insensate almost as soon as the smoke entered the respective bottles. First their legs, wings, and antennae stopped moving; then they keeled over. This done, Damián emptied the contents of the bottle traps into the kitchen trash can before taking a semimoldy piece of fish from the fridge and putting half of it in the trash and dropping the other half on the floor. Replacing the lid, he put his ear to the side of the trash can, listening for several minutes with heart in mouth until, one by one, he heard the renewed buzzing of the insects as they began to revive. In spite of appearances, the smoke had indeed only knocked them out, not killed them altogether.

The voice told him to take his time cleaning up the ash and the rest of the leftovers, and, recalling his meticulousness with manual tasks in his former life, he obeyed. He washed every last speck of ash down the drain, and threw the aluminum foil into the toilet in little scrunched-up balls. One flush and it all disappeared.

There was now the issue of the bottles, which he decided to cut up into small pieces, put inside a trash bag, and hide in the built-in wardrobe. Lastly, he aired the kitchen to clear out any residual smell of smoke, leaving the window open to suggest how the insects had gotten in. He then made his way back to his hiding place, with the sensation that it was increasingly much less troublesome to get into it, and far harder to get out.

Lying on his back on the makeshift bed, hands on stomach and eyes closed, he tried to conjure up O'Kane's old studio, but found he could not. This seemed decidedly strange to him. He then tried calling to mind the faces of his father and Chinese sister, but these, too, refused to appear, and he mentally asked Iñaki O'Kane if he was responsible for this amputation.

"It's a question of economy," the interviewer said, responding instantly. "Of conserving your energies for what's to come."

"What's to come?" Damián asked.

"A chain of events that you yourself have set in motion."

While he was now struggling to evoke certain mental images, his senses had become preposterously sharp. He could hear a phone ringing in a neighboring home, and pick out airborne smells, and thereby travel the length and breadth of the house with his eyes closed. For his whole being to have been honed to such a degree brought about a sensation of quiet euphoria, and of safety, which, in turn, cleared a space for him in the universe, one he'd never had before.

As EVENING FELL, Damián heard the familiar rumble and scrape of the garage door, and was immediately put on high alert. Peering into the wardrobe darkness, he listened as the car pulled into the garage, as its engine cut out, and then its doors were opened and shut. Fede and Paula had returned together once more, and, far away though they were, he was able to make out their voices quite clearly. He followed their movements, turning his head in a twitchy birdlike fashion, trying to catch as much as he could of their conversation. They mounted the four steps from the garage to the door in the hall; there came the sound of the key in the lock, then that of the pair making their way along the hall. . . . Hearing, as acute as his was now, was almost a kind of seeing.

The lovers, still clearly hungry for each other, came straight to the bedroom, where the verbal sparring commenced, only to be cut short by Fede, who was asking what the terrible smell was.

"The ghost, probably," Paula joked.

"Ghosts don't smell like rotting food," said the man. "It must be coming from the kitchen; we didn't clean up in there after all. Give me a minute."

"Not a second more," Paula said.

Damián heard the man go off down the hall. An instant then followed in which reality briefly ceased its usual forward motion, like the sun momentarily falling dark. Damián filled this lull with a very clear picture of Fede as he unwittingly opened the trash can, reaching into the bag to find the cord hidden around its edge, as yet unaware of the angry swarm inside, which, as Damián had foreseen, would take the man's incursion as an attack. Moments later, the lull came to a definitive end as Fede began to howl, the noise starting in the kitchen but passing rapidly back along the hall and reverberating around the entire house. Damián guessed that by the time Fede reached the bedroom, he would have sustained numerous stings—to his face, perhaps to his neck, and certainly on his hands. He sounded less like a person about to be condemned than one whose sentence had already come down and who was begging for the coup de grâce to be called off.

"Wasps! Wasps!" he wailed.

"What?" Paula cried. "Where's your injector, the antidote?"

"There're too many; they're all over me! Call an ambulance!"

Damián closed his eyes, funneling his entire being down into his auditory sense, and, remarkably, "saw" with his ears how Fede, still swiping at the air, launched himself onto the bed, while Paula ran pell-mell around the house, utterly unable to act with anything approximating decisiveness. He also "saw" her expression as the crazy questions beset her: How, how could the fate she had imagined befalling Lucía have happened to Fede? If the police came, and saw evidence of nefarious activity, would she be the prime suspect? Should she make a run for it? Or would that only make her more of a suspect?

The whole incident took mere seconds to unfold, but each second went on and on, tangibly stretching and distorting, as though comprising an entirely new, physical substance. And as Paula tore around the house, trying to work out what to do, the little squadron of wasps went on attacking Fede, over and over, as he writhed about on the bed, attempting to protect himself with the sheets.

"Are you getting all of this?" said the voice. "Can you hear?"

"I'm seeing it with my ears," Damián said, astonished at this newly acquired faculty, the result, he assumed, of his famished state, and doubtless something with which all his ghostly brethren were endowed.

Indeed, he was able to pick out the flight of the wasps, situating each and every one as they flew about the space. They fell upon their victim repeatedly, since, unlike the stingers of bees, theirs were not barbed and went in and out of the victim's flesh with ease. The savaging seemed to reach a crescendo, but then continued at that pitch for a phenomenal amount of time, before eventually tailing off. The wasps, which during the attack had acted like a single organism, began to disperse, which Damián also "saw," again with his ears. They shot apart like a ball of fireworks, transforming into tiny shooting stars that scattered around the rooms of the house.

At a certain point, the only sound to be heard was Fede's agonized panting. Another lull ensued before the sound of approaching sirens struck up outside, of ambulances, and fire trucks, and even perhaps the police, followed by the entrance of a dozen or more people who came rushing into the bedroom. Damián "saw" the comings and goings of the chaotic army of emergency workers, and "saw" Paula's manic attempt to explain; she herself, though not in tears, was having trouble breathing, and could hardly get her words out.

"We've got to stabilize him," said a man.

"Not much left here to stabilize," said a woman.

This exchange took place with the two individuals leaving the bedroom, Fede doubtless being taken on a stretcher to the mobile ICU Damián pictured parked out front.

"This is the third wasp call we've had," said another man, in all likelihood a firefighter. "It's hardly even summer yet."

"'When wasps are in flight, winter will bite,'"

came a reply from someone standing very close to the wardrobe.

"I've combed the place, no nests," said a third male voice from somewhere by the bedroom door. "But the kitchen window's open, and there were food scraps all over the place. The trash bag was on the floor, and the trash itself had spilled out. There was a moldy bit of fish in there; most likely they were chowing down on that. Then the poor sucker went to take the trash bag out. That'll do it."

It was deeply pleasing to Damián, as an avowed admirer of user manuals, to see theory and practice in such seamless alignment once again.

18

SOON AFTER Fede was taken away and Paula's simultaneous departure, and following the withdrawal of the firefighters, as well, the area of the house closest to Damián's cave was invaded by another group of professionals. He discerned four voices: two belonging to men, and two to women. He heard them moving about the space, shifting furniture around, opening cupboards. Instructions were given, and observations on the state of the house bandied about. Finally, the man who seemed to be in charge of the unit and one of the women came into the master bedroom itself and began sizing up the space. The man opened the antique wardrobe, beyond which Damián's hiding place was located, and slid some of the clothes on hangers from side to side.

"I tell you, this is a nothing job: nothing to see, nothing to do. Window open, trash can not properly closed, half a moldy fish inside, and some idiot with an allergy rolling around with his lover while his wife's off visiting her sick mom. Pretty despicable, don't you think? Look at the state of this bedroom; it reeks of cum."

He heard the woman *hmm* absentmindedly, as though absorbed in some task, though what precisely, Damián could not guess. The man he presumed to be her superior closed the antique wardrobe again before heading over to the door.

"We've contacted the wife," said the woman, "and she's on her way back. If you aren't going to order the place sealed, she'll be back here either tonight or in the morning—but look at what she's going to be walking into. I feel for her, personally. At least give me a hand shaking out these sheets."

"Have you lost your mind? Come on, let's get out of here. I've still got to fill in the report, and I'm supposed to be going to a meeting at my kids' school."

A few minutes later, the quartet was gone, leaving the house in silence. Damián stayed where he was a further half hour, to be on the safe side, before climbing out and doing a tour of the house, mentally totting up all the damage incurred. The place was even more of a mess following the interventions of the police and the firefighters, but by his calculations he had a good four or five hours before Lucía and María might be back.

He started cleaning in the kitchen, and worked at a leisurely pace. It had been quite a while now since he'd felt any need to hurry, though he still remembered the sensation, in the same way he could remember the pounds he had lost, which had dropped off his body, disappearing down some invisible drain. A ghost, he said to himself as he began gathering up plates and dishes, has all the time in the world. The word *world* brought to mind the song his mother used to like, "A Funny Old World," and he began to hum the tune as he loaded the dishwasher.

The world, which was still without any adequate comparison, had indeed been a funny old place. And it remained so—in a sense, that was its defining characteristic, though a little less so since Damián had found his place in it. That the place in question should be a built-in wardrobe, hidden behind another, antique wardrobe, made the situation interesting in a purely biological sense. He had become a kind of spider, he thought, occupying some dusty corner, and controlling the motions of the universe, unseen. He smiled at the idea.

He turned on the dishwasher, and, still humming to himself, dealt with the pieces of crockery too large to fit in the dishwasher, washing them by hand. The melody, by now a kind of canticle, helped

him to think. Given the circumstances, it was altogether possible that a friend or relative might walk
in at any moment, coming with the same intention
as his: to restore order to the house before mother
and daughter returned. All the same, it seemed
unlikely. Lucía would place her trust in him, Ghost
Butler, secure perhaps in the knowledge—or even
only the intuition—that Fede's death had been his
doing, and she would leave him to it.

He stopped, closed his eyes, and, scouring
pad in his right hand and pan in his left, entered
Lucía's head in the same way a hacker gains
access to someone else's computer. To Damián, it
seemed that, though affected by the episode, she
was thankful to have been liberated from her husband. Before she had any chance to notice this
alien presence in her mind, Damián slipped back
out, with all the care he took when slipping out of
the wardrobe, while simultaneously making a note
of the means he had used to gain access. Sergio
O'Kane and Iñaki Gabilondo both came to mind;
the renown they had provided him was more or
less banal in comparison with Ghost Butler's noto-
riety. This was a fame whose beneficiary was per-
manently absent. Probably the most famous being
in the universe to remain totally unseen—barring

one or two slips—was God. That was power: the ability to act from the shadows.

Having seen to the kitchen, and straightened the furniture in the living room, he swept all the rooms and vacuumed the hallway. Everywhere else was untouched, save for the master bedroom and bathroom. He went in, avoiding turning on any lights—not wishing to alert the neighbors—though it was dark outside now, and stripped the bed, taking sheets and pillowcases, along with the clothes strewn about the place, and putting them in the washing machine. He put on rubber gloves and cleaned the toilet, the bathroom sink, and the bathtub before making the bed with clean sheets and vacuuming the carpet. He observed the room in the half-light of the streetlamps outside. His work was done, the place looked good as new, and it was not yet midnight. Most likely, he thought, Lucía and María were spending the night in a hotel or at the house of a relative, and would not appear until the next day.

He went back to the kitchen, took a banana out of the fridge, and sat down to eat it in the living room. He chose the spot facing the television but didn't dare turn it on. A short while later, he was back in the master bedroom, where he lay down on the bed, on Lucía's side, and turned on the radio, waiting for the next news bulletin. And Fede's case had indeed been picked up by local reporters. The body was currently in the hands of the Forensics Service, awaiting an autopsy. The presenter, after a comment to all allergy sufferers and to the public in general that because of the last warm winter there were more wasps around this year than usual, briefly interviewed a firefighter, who gave some advice on what to do if anyone came across a wasps' nest.

Damián guessed the autopsy would not take place until the next day, and that it would be a further day or so before the burial or cremation. Turning off the radio, he got up from the bed, and wondered if it would be prudent to take a shower. He decided to run the risk, and afterward he gave himself a haircut and a shave, lopping off the castaway beard and flushing the clippings down the toilet. The face that appeared in the mirror was that of a stranger, someone he had never met before, but for whom he felt an immediate fondness.

"You and I are going to get along just fine," he said.

Having thus cleaned himself up, he opened the middle door to the antique wardrobe, parted the hangers, and stepped through the concealed panel into his den. He fell asleep with knees to chest,

in the fetal position, imagining himself not yet
born and still in the maternal womb, but with his
head already pointed down, as though the happy
moment were imminent. He repeated those words
to himself: *the happy moment.*

19

LUCÍA AND THE GIRL came back to the house midway through the next morning. Lucía's mother was with them, and she set up in the guest room. They had spent the night in a hotel or at a relative's house, Damián guessed. He heard them walking around the house, either saying nothing or speaking in very quiet voices indeed, as though at a wake, thought Damián, although nothing here felt particularly wakeful. Lucía's mother spoke a little more loudly at points, when making a practical suggestion or referring to something logistical, but the heavy morguelike atmosphere soon came down again to crush all conversation. The ghost heard them exclaim at the sparkling cleanliness of the rooms; it appeared that Lucía had been prepared for a total disaster area, since that was how the firefighters had described it. She also mentioned that this information had come to her via some women with whom she worked.

"Who was that?" asked her daughter.

"It doesn't matter," said the mother, her tone sharp. "You don't know them."

Damián heard them enter the bedroom and stop, from what he could tell, in front of the antique wardrobe.

"My parents' wardrobe!" cried the grandmother.

"Like I told you," Lucía said.

"And you're sure it's theirs?"

"Definitely. Have a look down here . . . the marks. Look, those are mine, and those are Jorge's."

"Don't you find it a little sinister, honey, having it here?"

"Quite the opposite, Mamá. I like its presence."

Damián heard, or sensed, as one of them, probably the grandmother, opened the middle door and leaned her head inside.

"Strange smell," she said.

"That's the air freshener Fede brought. I've gotten rid of it now."

"And what about the ghost?" the grandmother said with a smile, which Damián glimpsed through the edge of the hidden door.

"What ghost?" Lucía asked.

"The one that haunts the wardrobe."

"Oh, that was nothing. A silly idea I had. At first, when the wardrobe arrived, it brought so many

memories of Grandpa and Grandma to mind. . . .
It was to do with that."

The door to the antique wardrobe closed again
and mother and daughter went away, out of the bedroom and down the hall, to the far end of the house.

The rest of the day passed uneventfully, though
both the doorbell and phone rang almost constantly. People phoning to offer condolences,
thought Damián, and the typical callers come to
express support for widow and newly orphaned
child. And yet the overwhelming sensation was
one of calm; it pervaded every corner of the house,
the ghost's refuge included.

Lucía got into bed early. Damián listened to
her every move from the second she came in and
closed the door behind her. By way of the new
internal vision that his brain had spontaneously
developed, he translated every sound into an
image. He saw her as she sat down on the bed,
directly in front of the antique wardrobe, and continued watching as she looked at herself for several minutes in the old mirror with its mottling of
silver oxide stains. And he continued to see her as
she went in to the bathroom; he saw her close the
door, saw as she sat on the toilet, her gaze distant.
He watched as she brushed her teeth, removed
her makeup—possibly—got undressed, and left

her clothes on the side of the bidet, and watched as she put her hair up to avoid getting it wet and then stepped into the shower. He watched her come back into the bedroom, untuck the sheets, get into the bed, and turn off the light.

Listening to the way she breathed, it was clear to him that she was yearning for something. Damián's mind turned to Fede, whose body the family would collect the next day from the Forensics Service. The autopsy would be complete by now, and the only thing they would have found was the poison administered by the stingers of thirty or so angry wasps. But did Fede's memory not deserve at least a few days' respite? Of course not.

Nevertheless, Damián waited a few minutes more, allowing his former life to pass before his eyes—in the same way a drowning person is said to see such a sequence of images. Then the birth began. He opened the hidden door, climbed into the antique wardrobe, bisecting Lucía's clothes on his way out, as though they were the mucous membranes he had to traverse to reach the ghost life that awaited him. He opened the middle door of the antique wardrobe, and heard a moan from Lucía. She was lying on her side, with her legs drawn up. Damián said, It's me, no need to worry, and, stepping out of the tracksuit, he slipped between the sheets behind her, merging with her just as music and lyrics merge. There was nothing to it, he thought, and yet at the same time it was a far subtler thing than he had imagined. Then, inside his head, he heard the voice.

"You've arrived," it said.

"Arrived where?" asked Damián.

"Wherever you want to be," said the voice.

And that was all.

BELLEVUE LITERARY PRESS is devoted to publishing
literary fiction and nonfiction at the intersection of
the arts and sciences because we believe that science
and the humanities are natural companions for
understanding the human experience.
With each book we publish, our goal is to foster a
rich, interdisciplinary dialogue that will forge new
tools for thinking and engaging with the world.

To support our press and its mission, and for our
full catalogue of published titles, please visit us
at blpress.org.

BELLEVUE LITERARY PRESS
New York